# DAKOTA KNOX
# LONDON,
# LOVE,
# & TERROR

BOOK 2

This is a work of fiction. Names, characters, organizations, places, events, and incidents are either products of the author's imagination or are used fictitiously.

## DAKOTA KNOX: LONDON, LOVE, AND TERROR

ISBN: Paperback: 9798838157386

Cover design and interior layout by the author.
Printed in the United States of America.

DAKOTA KNOX
# LONDON,
# LOVE,
# & TERROR

BOOK 2

## CHARLIE H. CAMPBELL

# FACTS:

- All descriptions of archaeological artifacts
- References to events in the Bible, the writings of Flavius Josephus, and other historians

# CHAPTER 1
## Tuesday, June 21, Haslemere, England.

Radomir Lucic slammed his phone back into its cradle on his office desk. "That teenage scum. I want Dakota Knox killed!"

He thrust his chair backward, stood, and kicked the Rottweiler that was lying next to him. "Out of my way, you stupid dog." He walked to the window overlooking the **rolling green hills** of his estate thirty-nine miles southwest of London. Breathing slowly through his congested nose, he turned to his assistant Ahmed and bodyguard Eeman. "I want Dakota Knox terminated at any cost. Make it your highest priority."

"What happened?" Ahmed asked.

"The young man we smuggled out of Israel just informed me that Dakota's on a plane coming to London."

"Avner told you that?"

"Yes."

"Where *is* Avner?"

"He's here. He's unpacking my new artifacts."

"So Dakota's on a flight to London, and he's landing today?" Eeman asked.

"No, Eeman. He's on a plane coming to London, but it's going to circle the city for a few days. *Of course, today.*"

Eeman said, "Maybe he's just coming to do a little sightseeing, Boss."

Radomir shook his head in disbelief. "You're a fool, Eeman. He's coming to England because he's been tipped off somehow. And he wants to find the other artifacts and collect the reward money."

"Oh, wow." Eeman said. "He's smart."

Radomir pounded his fist on his oak desk. "No. He's not smart. He's a money-hungry, fame-seeking nuisance. If he was smart, he would have stayed in Israel and enjoyed the summer like a normal teenager."

"Uh, Boss, you had a sniper try to kill him last week while he was surfing."

"Well, yes, I did, Eeman. Because if that piece of garbage tracks us down, we're all going to jail. And the sniper would have taken him out if it wasn't for that dumb girl who rescued him."

"The girl that drove the Ford Bronco up the beach?" Eeman asked.

"Yes. And I want her dead too. Avner got a message from Gershom Haddad, whose wife is on the plane. And she said that girl is sitting next to Dakota."

"That girl's a babe." Eeman said. "I saw her picture on that news show and—"

"Did you get the airline they're on?" Ahmed asked.

Radomir batted away a fly that landed on his shaven head,

grabbed a piece of paper on his desk, and turned it to Ahmed. "British Airways. Flight number 166."

Ahmed tapped the number into a flight-tracker app on his phone. "Grab your gun, Eeman. They're scheduled to land at Heathrow soon. But they'll have to clear customs and probably wait for bags. We might be able to get there in time."

Eeman jumped to his feet. "Woo! Let's go!"

Ahmed put out his cigarette in the ashtray on Radomir's desk. "We'll let you know what happens, Boss."

"Go! Do it clean, please. Avoid cameras."

"We always do," Ahmed said.

"Not that one time," Eeman said. "Remember that time, Ahmed, at—"

"Shut!"

After the two men walked out, Radomir sat in his leather recliner. The fly that had been annoying him landed on Dagon, the Rottweiler that had laid back down by his chair. Radomir reached for his electric fly swatter, whacked the fly, and held it down against Dagon's head while the fly sizzled and smoked.

Radomir chuckled. "You messed with the wrong person, you little germ-infested maggot with wings. And soon enough, that seventeen-year-old surfer boy from California will realize the same."

# Chapter 2
## Tuesday, June 21, 30,000 feet above Europe.

Dakota Knox tilted his British Airways seat back and nodded off. The article about fun things to do in London had put him to sleep. His hand slowly slipped out of Afton's. She looked at him and smiled, glad that he was able to sleep on the flight, something she was rarely able to do.

Afton turned and peered through the window at the tiny cities somewhere in Western Europe. She picked up her phone. There was a message from her good friend, Lily.

> **Lily:** What's up girl? How are you? My mom said you nearly died in Israel.

> **Afton:** Hey Lils! I'm doing great. But yes, I had a close call last week with a madman who was shooting at a friend. It's a long story, but I'm fine. Wasn't injured at all. How are you?

> **Lily:** I'm good, but you've got to give me more details.

> **Afton:** Well, I'm flying home right now. So I can give you all the details next time I see you. But I met this really sweet guy named Dakota. Our dads are working together in Israel this summer.

> **Lily:** Is he a Christian?

**Afton:** He loves Jesus more than anyone I know.

**Lily:** Wow. Is he cute?

Afton turned and looked at his sun-tanned face and messy light brown hair. *Melt my heart, Dakota.*

**Afton:** Gorgeous.

**Lily:** Sounds like a keeper.

**Afton:** We were having the best time getting to know each other and exploring Israel. But there was a heist at the museum in Jerusalem. Maybe you heard about it in the news. The thieves stole a bunch of archaeological artifacts. And Dakota and I and some of his sibs figured out who did it.

**Lily:** No way!

**Afton:** Yeah, and Dakota recovered one of the artifacts! But then someone, probably one of the thieves, tried to shoot him while he was surfing last Thursday. Really crazy!

**Lily:** Oh my goodness Afton! That's insane. Is he okay?

**Afton:** He's fine. But that's why we're flying home. It's too dangerous to stay in Israel. We'll go back if the thieves are caught.

**Lily:** Wow. Okay. Let's get together when you're able.

**Afton:** Let's! I'd love for you to meet Dakota.

**Lily:** Wait. He's coming with you?

**Afton:** Yes, and his family. They'll be staying in a house they rented down the street from us.

**Lily:** I can't wait to meet him. He sounds like a great guy. Does he live in Israel?

**Afton:** No. California. San Diego.

**Lily:** That would be a really long distant relationship.

**Afton:** Well, we will be at the same university this fall. I have a lot to update you on.

**Lily:** If it doesn't work out with Dakota, I found out yesterday that Dylan Cooper likes you.

**Afton:** Dylan from church?

**Lily:** Yeah, the cute guy in the college group. You've talked to him.

**Afton:** Oh wow. He seems like a great guy. How'd you find out?

**Lily:** His friend told me.

**Afton:** Okay, thanks for letting me know Lils. Let's talk more later this week.

**Lily:** Miss you Afton! See ya soon.

A few minutes later, the plane encountered some turbulence, and Dakota stirred. He opened his eyes and turned toward Afton. "I guess I fell asleep."

"That's good. You probably needed a nap."

"I had a crazy dream. Wait. Did you tell me that you've decided to go to Liberty University this fall, or did I dream that?"

Afton smiled. "I think you dreamt that."

"Oh wow. No, really?"

Afton couldn't hold back the truth. "I told you that."

"It wasn't a dream?"

"Not a dream."

"Oh, good. Did you tell me you want to be an archaeologist?"

"I did."

"Were we holding hands before I fell asleep?"

"You must have dreamt that part," Afton said.

"Seriously?"

"I'm kidding. We *were* holding hands until you fell asleep."

"Oh, good."

The pilot's voice came on overhead. "Good afternoon. This is your captain speaking. Air traffic control at London Heathrow put us into a holding pattern. There are too many planes coming in at the same time. So, they've asked us to circle the airport for what will probably be an extra ten to fifteen minutes. So, we're going to do that. We'll have you on the ground soon. Thanks for flying British Airways. Welcome to London."

"No worries," Afton said. "We're not in a hurry."

Dakota raised his seat back. "Do you know who's picking us up at the airport?"

"My uncle, Chad. He's borrowing a 15-passenger van from his work."

"That's nice of him."

Afton leaned toward Dakota and whispered, "Are you still going to talk to that lady who questioned you earlier?"

"Yeah. I don't *know* that she's related to the chief of security at the museum. But her last name makes me suspicious."

# Chapter 3
## Tuesday, June 21, Heathrow Airport, London.

After circling the Heathrow airport for about fifteen minutes, the British Airways jet touched down and parked at the gate. Dakota stood and opened the overhead bin.

"Can I get your rollaboard down for you, Afton?"

"Please. Thank you. It's the one with the pink ribbon on it."

Dakota glanced back at the woman who had recognized him from the press conference at the Israel Museum. Her last name, Haddad, was the same as the chief of security at the museum who had never followed up on Dakota's tip.

As the Knox and Hansley families walked through the terminal, Dakota and Afton slowed down and allowed their moms and siblings to pass.

Dakota's fourteen-year-old brother Hank was looking at his phone and bumped into him. "Why are you walking so slow, Dak?"

"I'll tell you later. Stay with Mom."

As the woman drew near, Dakota said, "Excuse me. You stopped by my seat earlier."

"Yes, I remember."

"I overheard the flight attendant say your last name, *Haddad*. You wouldn't happen to know a *Gershom* Haddad, would you?"

"Gershom? No. Why do you ask?"

"Well, I know a Gershom Haddad, and I thought maybe you were related."

"I don't know a Gershom. I'm sorry."

"Okay, no worries. Thank you."

As Dakota and Afton walked off, he whispered, "She said she doesn't know a Gershom."

"I heard. Haddad is probably a common last name in Israel."

The Knoxes and Hansleys retrieved their checked baggage, cleared customs, and walked into the massive Arrivals Hall. It

was bustling with thousands of travelers. Afton's uncle Chad was waiting for them. After introductions were made and hugs exchanged, he led them toward the doors.

Dakota noticed that one of his shoes was untied. "I'll catch up." As he tied his shoe, he saw Mrs. Haddad standing about ten feet away from him.

A young lady approached her and said, "It is so good to see you. How was your flight? I'm sorry that Gershom couldn't come with you."

*Gershom! She lied to me.* Dakota couldn't hear the woman's response. He straightened up and glared at her until she noticed. She turned away, and Dakota hurried off to catch up to Afton.

"I just heard a lady giving Mrs. Haddad a hug, and she said, 'I'm sorry *Gershom* couldn't come with you.' She lied, Afton. She *does* know a Gershom. I think she's the wife of the chief of security at the Israel Museum. But why wouldn't she want me to know she was related to Gershom? Something fishy is going on with that guy. I think he might have helped steal the artifacts."

"You think?"

"We know Avner, the other employee at the museum, was in on the heist."

"We do. And if Gershom was in on it, and his wife was on the plane, and she seemed nervous that you were coming to England . . . Oh, wow, Dakota. This is very interesting, but—"

"It is."

"But we came to England to avoid any more trouble with these guys."

"You're right," Dakota said. "I need to stay out of it."

"Right. The detectives can work on the case."

"Exactly."

• • •

On the highway, a couple of miles from Heathrow airport, Eeman twisted a silencer onto the barrel of his Smith & Wesson .45 caliber handgun. "If we spot them—poom, poom! Two shots and we're off. Airport custodians can clean up the mess."

Ahmed nodded in agreement as he weaved Radomir's black BMW M760 around slow-moving cars.

Eeman held up his phone. "Here's a photo of Dakota. Sandy light brown hair, blue eyes, six-foot-two-inches-tall, seventeen years old."

"I know what he looks like!"

"And here's the girl. Same color hair, a little lighter, hangs below her shoulders a bit, five-foot-eleven or so. Green eyes. Cute face."

"All right, stop drooling," Ahmed said. "There's no arrival curb for picking up people at Heathrow, so we'll have to pull into the short-term parking lot."

"What terminal are they arriving at?"

"Terminal five. Once we park, we'll monitor the foot traffic coming out of the Arrivals Hall. If we spot them, we'll let them make their way toward their car, and we'll come in from behind them."

Eeman pulled back the slide on his gun and loaded a round into the chamber. "That works for me."

# Chapter 4
## Tuesday, June 21, Heathrow Airport, London.

Afton's uncle Chad led the family out the door of the Arrivals Hall and toward the short-term parking lot. "Follow me, everybody. The van is over this way in short-term parking."

When they found the white Mercedes 15-passenger van, Chad and Dakota loaded the suitcases and Dakota's surfboard and guitar into the back. Chad backed the van out of the parking spot.

"Wow. This van's amazing," Dakota's mom Abigail said. "All these seats and room for bags. Thank you, Chad, for picking us up. Very nice of you."

"You're welcome. The van belongs to the hotel I manage."

Chad looked at the Knox and Hansley families in the rearview mirror. "We should have you to Marylebone in a little while."

Dakota's ten-year-old sister Jalynn said, "I thought we were going to London."

"Marylebone is a district . . . a neighborhood on the west side of London," Afton explained. "It's where we live."

A few minutes later, Dakota noticed that Chad kept looking in his mirrors.

After another minute of mirror-checking, Chad sped up and got over a lane. "Go around me, you spaz!"

Afton's mom Nicola asked, "Is there a problem, Chad?"

"Some guy in a black BMW is tailgating us. I think I cut him off a couple of minutes ago. Now, he appears a bit unhinged."

"These vans are great for large groups," Nicola said to Abigail, "but they're hard to drive around big cities. It's easy to cut people off."

"I'm sorry, Knox family," Chad said. "There are some crazy drivers in London, but he's passing us now."

Dakota looked over Afton's shoulder through the tinted side window. The black BMW was next to them, going the same speed. The male passenger looked Middle Eastern with black curly hair. He was motioning with his hand for Chad to pull over.

"Maybe he's not mad, and we're just dragging a piece of luggage behind the van or something," Hank said.

Nicola agreed. "Perhaps he's telling us to pull over to fix something, Chad."

Dakota recalled his surfboard dragging next to the Bronco after Afton rescued him on the beach. He turned around to make sure his new board was still in the van. *Phew! It's still there.*

Jalynn said, "Maybe the back of the van is on fire!"

Afton's eleven-year-old sister Evelyn shrieked.

Her brother Ethan said, "Calm down, the van's not on fire."

"Chad," Nicola said. "Why don't you just pull over at the next off-ramp and check on the van."

"I can do that."

Dakota thought *that's a terrible idea!*

Chad put on his blinker to exit the highway.

Dakota looked out the window to watch how the BMW driver would react. The driver quickly slowed down and swerved behind the van to follow them off the exit.

Dakota couldn't hold back his thoughts any longer. "Chad, it's not my place to tell you how to drive—I've only had my license for a year, but I would not stop the van. These guys are definitely mad. If they were alerting us to a problem with the van, they would have kept driving when we pulled off the highway."

"I think you're right, Dakota."

"If you get out of the car," Dakota continued, "they're probably going to be violent."

"You sound like someone who's seen some road-rage incidents in southern California."

"Oh, we have!" Jalynn said.

"Drivers in So Cal are psycho," Hank said. "We feel right at home."

"All right, I won't pull over. I'll try to lose them. Everyone buckled up? Nicola, if they follow me around this next turn, call the police, and alert them to what's going on. Hold on, everybody!"

"This is awesome!" Ethan said.

Chad pressed the gas pedal. Dakota could hear the Mercedes six-cylinder diesel engine working hard.

"This isn't the Batmobile," Hank said to Ethan. "What does this thing do—like 60?"

Afton squeezed Dakota's arm and whispered, "Welcome to London."

"Thanks," Dakota said. "We'll be fine."

Chad made a right turn, and the black BMW followed. "Call the police!" He sped up and looked in his mirror. "How we're going to lose a BMW in a 15-passenger van, I do not know."

"If this was the Batmobile," Ethan said, "we could just activate the rear taser defenses and incinerate that thing."

"Not helpful right now, Ethan!" Chad said.

The Mercedes van raced through a neighborhood.

"Hello, police?" Nicola said into her phone. "Thank God you answered. We are being chased by two men in a black BMW . . . yes . . . no . . . I think we cut them off, and they are trying to run us off the road . . . we are currently driving northbound on—"

The van hit a dip in the road, and Nicola's phone flew out of her hand. "Dang it!"

Chad yanked the steering wheel to make a left turn. "Sorry, everybody!"

Dakota heard the tires stressing under the weight and speed. He turned and looked out the window. The BMW was still on their trail. "Uh, Chad, they're coming up on your side."

The BMW was racing alongside the van. The driver rubbed the side of his car against the van and was trying to force it to crash into the parked cars on the side of the road. Several of the Knoxes and Hansleys yelled.

"We're going to crash!"

"Chad!"

"Hold on!"

"We're dead!"

Chad swerved the van back into the BMW, forcing the driver to slow down and pull back. "Those idiots! I mean, seriously, I accidentally cut someone off, and he wants to run us off the road. What's the world coming to?" When Chad checked his mirror, the van drifted slightly to the right and tore off a parked car's side mirror. "Sorry about that, whoever's car that was!"

Nicola yelled, "Chad, don't get us killed. Slow down!"

"We're getting close to your neighborhood. I've got to lose them."

Nicola agreed.

Fifty yards in front of them was a yellow light. There was no way Chad would make it through before it turned red. "Perfect," he said. He floored the gas pedal and raced through the red light, barely avoiding the cars coming from the other direction.

Chad looked in his mirror. The driver of the BMW was forced to stop at the red light. "Ha! Lost them. Phew. That was close. Sorry about that, everybody. My goodness. Okay, I'll make a couple more turns, and they'll never find us."

Everyone breathed easier.

"Wow. Well, Knoxes, welcome to London." Nicola said. "I trust that will be the peak of the drama while you're here. I'm sorry about the van, Chad. Will insurance cover the scratches?"

"It'll be covered, not a problem."

"Okay, good. We can pay the deductible. The Knoxes are staying in a flat on the same block as ours, so if you can find a place to park anywhere by our place, that would be great."

# Chapter 5

Dakota stepped out of the van and looked around. He had already noticed that London was an enormous, crowded city. But the block Afton lived on seemed quiet and peaceful. The street was lined with elegant five-story brick townhomes built right next to each other. Across the street was a narrow rectangular park that stretched the length of the block.

Afton said, "This is my neighborhood."

"It's really cool," Dakota said.

"I like it."

"How long have you lived here?"

"Since I was five, so twelve years."

"I like all the trees," Dakota said as he helped unload the suitcases from the back of the van.

"Aren't they lovely?" Nicola said. "Most of those are London plane trees. But there are Japanese maple, cherry, and lilac, too. We love them."

After her uncle drove off, Afton said, "Message me, Dakota, after you guys get settled into your flat. I think we're all going out to dinner tonight, seeing that our refrigerators will be empty."

"Sounds good. I'll text you soon."

As the Knoxes took the elevator up to the fourth floor, Hank said, "I heard Afton mention dinner tonight. I counted about ten different places within the last mile."

"We'll get you fed, Hank," Abigail said. "Let's check out the apartment first."

"Do I get my own room, Mom?" Jalynn inquired.

"I think so. There are three bedrooms." Abigail opened the door. The afternoon sun filled the living room and kitchen with warm golden light.

"Wow. This place is great," Dakota said. "Looks just like the photos you showed us."

"I love these large windows and the view of the park and trees," Abigail said. "And we're high enough up that we shouldn't hear the cars. This apartment is fabulous."

"Is there any food in the fridge?" Hank asked as he headed toward the kitchen. "You know, Mom, we're on Israel's time, two hours ahead. So technically, it's about six p.m., which is dinner—"

"Hank, we flew first class, and they fed us on the plane. Relax." Dakota said.

"No food. The fridge is spotless. Can you make anything with baking soda, Mom? Soup or something?"

"Dakota, I saw that you talked to a lady on the plane who stopped by your seat," Abigail said.

"Yeah, she recognized me from one of the news shows. She stopped by to thank me for helping find the David Inscription. But I don't know, Mom. Her last name was Haddad. I asked her if she knew a Gershom Haddad, the chief of security at the Israel Museum, and she said no. But then I heard her friend at the airport say that she was sad Gershom couldn't join her."

"Oh."

"So, I don't know why she would lie to me unless she was nervous about her husband or me."

"Hmm. Well, there's nothing to worry about. The case of the missing artifacts is in competent hands. You don't need to try to figure it all out. Let the detectives in Israel do their job."

"Yeah, I did my part."

"We're here in London now. It's going to be a great time. And I love that we're so close to the Hansleys."

"Speaking of the Hansleys," Dakota said, "Afton told me some exciting news on our flight."

"Oh, yeah?"

"She wants to be an archaeologist. Seeing all those artifacts and sites in Israel was life-changing for her. So, she's changing her major from business to ancient history and archaeology."

"Wow."

"Well, here's the big news. She asked if I'd mind if she went to Liberty University this fall. She wants to learn from professors who have a Christian worldview."

"What did you tell her?"

"I said, I'd *love* for her to go to Liberty. Mom, I really like her."

"I know you do."

"You do?"

"I saw all the fun you guys were having in Israel."

"I've never liked anyone this much, Mom. And I was sad we were going to have to say goodbye at the end of the summer. But now, we're going to see each other at school."

"Wow, Dakota, that's amazing. Her parents are supportive?"

"She said they are."

"Well, your father and I certainly like her. She loves the Lord. She's smart, adventurous, beautiful inside and out. She seems like a wonderful girl for you."

"I agree. She's the kind of girl I hoped to find someday. I'm blown away."

"Do you think she likes you?"

Hank walked back into the room. "Who, Afton? She for sure likes you, Dak. She drove up the beach in that Bronco that was getting shot to pieces to save your life. I'd say she *loves* you."

"Well, I don't know about that," Dakota responded. "I think she would have done the same for you, Hank. But we *did* hold hands on the plane."

"You did?" Hank and Abigail said in unison.

"Yeah."

Jalynn walked into the living room. "You held Afton's hand? I saw it coming!"

Abigail looked at her phone. "Hold on, guys. Nicola is texting me about dinner. They're asking if we can meet outside in twenty minutes. I'll say yes. So, unpack your suitcases if you haven't. Hang up your clothes. And we'll go eat."

"Finally!" Hank said.

# Chapter 6
## Tuesday, June 21, Haslemere, England.

Ahmed pulled the BMW up to the massive black iron gate at the entrance to Radomir's estate. It slowly rolled open.

"Do you think Radomir's going to be mad about the scratches on his car?" Eeman asked.

"No. He has twelve cars. I'll send it to the body shop, and he won't even know it's gone. He'll be mad that we didn't knock off Dakota."

Ahmed drove the car up a cobblestone driveway that curved around enormous oak trees that dotted much of Radomir's land. At the top of the hill, the driveway circled a large stone fountain and perfectly manicured shrubs. Ahmed pulled the BMW into Radomir's garage, and the two men walked into the kitchen.

Radomir's chef Dario was at the stove cooking. "Ah, my friends! Welcome back to England. You returned from Israel today?"

"Yeah, we sailed into Portsmouth today. My legs are still wobbly." Eeman said. "We've missed your cooking, Dario."

"Thank you."

"What are you making?" Ahmed asked.

"Beef Stroganoff with mushrooms, pan-fried potatoes, a salad, and chocolate pecan bars for dessert. Dinner should be ready in about fifteen minutes."

"Oh, it's nice to be back," Eeman said. "I'm starving."

Ahmed set his wallet and gun down on the dining table. "It smells delicious, Dario. Do you know where Radomir's at?"

"He's in the Roman Empire Hall with Avner, arranging his new artifacts. He seemed happy a while ago. But his mood seems to have soured over the last few minutes—"

"Thanks. Come with me, Eeman."

They walked down the hall, and Ahmed peeked into the large room. It was one of four identically sized rooms in the mansion. The space looked like an exhibit hall at a museum. Twenty-four marble pedestals were evenly spaced in three rows throughout the room. Atop the pedestals were well-lit **Roman-era busts** of men and women, pots and bowls, weapons, and other ancient artifacts. The shelves and cases along the walls had countless more.

Ahmed could hear Radomir talking. "Angle the light more

to the right, Avner! And brighten it some."

"They're adjusting the lighting on **the Pilate stone**," Ahmed whispered to Eeman.

Radomir yelled, "Your dad is the museum's director, Avner! Didn't he teach you anything?"

"Well, I mainly just stood around and told people where—"

"Stop."

Ahmed leaned toward Eeman. "It doesn't seem like a good time to talk to him about Dakota."

"Is there ever a good time?" Eeman asked in a hushed voice.

"No. But over dinner might be better."

As they quietly backed away from the artifact hall, a woman opened a door near the end of the hallway and approached them. She had black hair pulled back in a ponytail and a handheld vacuum in her hand. When she looked up and saw Eeman and Ahmed, she said, "Eeman! You're back!"

Eeman held up his finger to shush her, but it was too late.

"Hi, Sabiya. It's good to see you, sis."

Sabiya was Eeman's younger sister. She had grown up in Iraq with him and was now Radomir's maid.

"How was your trip to Israel?"

Before Eeman could answer, Radomir said,

"Ah, my men. You're back. Come in. I trust you have some good news for me."

Eeman and Ahmed walked into the room.

"Not exactly," Ahmed said. "Please excuse us, Sabiya. We need to talk to Radomir privately."

Ahmed shut the door. "We spotted Dakota in the Heathrow parking structure. But it was too late to get a good shot at him."

"There were also cameras everywhere," Eeman said.

Ahmed continued. "So, we followed the van he was in and tried to force it off the road, but unfortunately, we weren't able. Then we got stuck at a red light. And they got away."

"Oh, that's very unfortunate."

Eeman said, "We drove around for about half an hour, Boss. But we couldn't find the van."

"But I *did* get the license plate number," Ahmed said. "I'll trace it to an address. We'll find him."

"You *will* find him," Radomir said. "I'm sure of that. He must be stopped."

# Chapter 7
## Tuesday, June 21, Marylebone, London.

The Knox and Hansley families met on the sidewalk for dinner. After a quick vote, they decided to go out for Thai food.

"Follow me," Nicola said. "It's only about a ten-minute walk to one of our favorite places."

Abigail said, "I love the yellow—"

"Curry," Hank said, finishing her sentence. "I love the yellow curry too, Mom, with chicken and—"

"Uh, actually, I was about to tell Mrs. Hansley that I love the yellowy-brown brickwork in the homes," Abigail said. "The whole neighborhood exudes charm and grace."

"Thank you," Nicola said. "We feel blessed to live here. This neighborhood surrounding the park is known as Bryanston Square. It feels safe, and it's about as tranquil as one can expect living this close to central London."

"It does seem tranquil. Very lovely," Abigail said.

"We can walk to just about anything—cafes, boutiques, coffee shops, bakeries, farmers' markets, the gym."

"Do you even need a car?"

"Hardly. We have a couple of cars, but there are several Tube stations close by," Nicola said.

"What's a tube?" Jalynn asked.

"A subway. An underground train," Dakota said.

"It's easier for my husband Steven to get to work on the Tube than driving and battling the traffic," Nicola said.

As the Knoxes and Hansleys walked along the well-manicured streets, Dakota and Afton drifted to the back of the group.

"How's your place?" Afton asked.

"We love it. It's totally nice. I mean, it's hard to beat the beach house in Israel. But it's great."

Afton tugged on Dakota's light blue hooded sweatshirt. "I'm glad you packed this. I forgot to tell you that it's definitely cooler here."

"I can feel the difference. For sure, a little chillier."

"Yeah, the average high temp in June is only about sixty-seven degrees."

"I can't believe we're in London," Dakota said.

"I'm delighted you guys came with us."

"So am I. It's wild how plans change. A couple of days ago, we were walking the streets of Jerusalem. And now, we're getting Thai food in London."

"Crazy. So, this is where I grew up," Afton said. "My primary school—"

She paused as a **double-decker bus** drove by. "My primary school is right over that way, and my secondary school is about

a five-minute walk over there. Our church is back that way."

"Primary and secondary. I think we would call that elementary school and high school in the states."

"Yes!"

"Speaking of schools," Dakota said, "I told my mom that you want to study history and archaeology instead of business and that you'd like to attend Liberty in September. She thought that was cool."

"I'm so glad to hear that," Afton said. "I wish Liberty was closer to your family in California. I like your mom and Hank and Jalynn. It would be fun to spend more time with them."

"Maybe they'll come back and visit Liberty while we're there."

As they continued walking, Dakota's hand bumped into Afton's. That reminded him that they had held hands on the plane and hadn't since. But now, he was nervous about reaching for it.

"I told my family that we held hands today on the plane," Dakota said.

Afton stopped walking and smiled at him. "You did? What was their reaction?"

"Well, Jalynn said she saw it coming. My mom seemed surprised. I've never told her that I've held a girl's hand."

"*Have* you held a girl's hand?"

They resumed walking.

"Yeah, like in elementary school, but not since then in any kind of romantic way. But my mom really likes you, Afton. So, she's happy about our friendship and that we'll be at the same school."

"Oh, that's a blessing to hear."

Dakota wondered, *should I reach for her hand again? Why am I so nervous about this? Afton said she was the happiest girl in the world on the plane when I held it earlier. But what if Hank or Jalynn turn around and see us holding hands and start laughing, and then Afton's mom turns around? That might shock Mrs. Hansley. Afton didn't tell me if she told her mom. . . . Maybe I'll just ask if I can hold it. . . . No, not now. Later.*

"Afton, would you mind if I . . . would you like to go out for dessert after Thai food? Just you and me?"

"I'd love that, Dakota."

"I like our brothers and sisters," Dakota said, "but it would be nice to hang out for a while, just you and me. Sort of like a date."

"Yeah, *like* a date, but not really a—"

"Well, no . . . I mean a *real* date."

"A real date. You're asking me out on a real date?"

"Yes!" Dakota said.

Afton looked at him with an adoring smile. "You're so sweet, Dakota. Yes, I'd love to go out with you on a real date."

"Cool. Pick your favorite place, and we'll go there."

"Okay. I'll think about it and let you know."

The families arrived at the Thai restaurant and sat down. Halfway through dinner, Dakota leaned over to his mom and whispered, "Afton and I would like to go out for dessert when dinner is over, just her and me. Is that okay with you?"

Abigail nodded yes.

When they were done eating, Dakota and Afton said bye to their families and walked in the opposite direction.

"I know a perfect place for dessert," Afton said. "It's about a fifteen-minute walk."

"Perfect."

As they walked, Dakota reached out his left hand. "May I hold your hand, Afton?"

Afton latched her hand onto his, looked over at him, and smiled. "I was hoping we would."

Dakota felt a wave of happiness sweep across him.

"I like your shoes," Dakota said.

Afton looked down at her light gray Vans with white stripes. "Oh, thanks. So, this restaurant we're going to has outdoor seating with a couple of fireplaces and little wood tables with candles on them. It's very charming."

"That sounds good," Dakota said. "I can't believe how light out it is."

"In June, the sun doesn't set until nine twenty or so."

"Wow. It goes down around eight in California."

As they walked, Dakota was struck by how different London was than Encinitas. The iconic red double-decker buses. The age and architectural styles of the buildings. The crowds of people. Narrow streets. Cars driving on the left side of the road. It all seemed so different. But the city became a blur walking next to Afton. *God, I can't believe I'm walking the streets of London with this girl . . . on a date. She's gorgeous. She loves You. Wow. How did this happen? You are so good to me. Bless our time together.*

"Whatcha thinkin' about Dakota?"

"You. I'm just super blessed to be with you, Afton."

"I'm blessed to be with you, Dakota."

"God is good!"

"He is!"

When they arrived at the restaurant, Dakota opened the

door for Afton. The hostess sat them at an outdoor table close to a large stone fireplace.

"What do you recommend, Afton?"

"I love their apple crumble with vanilla ice cream. The brown sugar, the buttery crisp crumble on top. It's heavenly."

"Sold."

As they enjoyed their dessert, Dakota said, "I love the live jazz band next door—they're good."

"They *are* good. But you know whose music I really like?"

"Coldplay?"

"I love Coldplay. They're doing a concert here soon. But no."

"Mat Kearney."

"Love him, but no."

"Need To Breathe."

"They're amazing, but no."

"I give up," Dakota said.

"You! You and your acoustic guitar. I loved leaving my window open at night in Israel, so I could listen to you play by the backyard fireplace."

"Oh, wow. Thanks. I didn't know you enjoyed it so much."

"It's my favorite, Dakota, especially when you'd sing worship songs. I could listen to that for hours. I'm glad you brought your guitar to England. How's your hand feeling, though? Are you able to play your guitar yet?"

Dakota showed her his hand that had been injured when the sniper's bullet hit the surfboard he was carrying. He moved his fingers around. "It's not all the way healed, but it feels a lot better than it did a couple of days ago."

"Good. I've been praying that God will bring total healing

to it."

"Thanks."

After every bit of the apple crumble was gone, Dakota noticed that Afton yawned.

"We should probably head back, you think? It's midnight in Israel."

"That would explain why I'm getting sleepy," Afton said.

They stood and began walking back to Bryanston Square.

"The streets are definitely quieter now," Afton said as she reached for Dakota's hand.

"How far is it back to your house?" Dakota inquired.

"About a mile walk."

"Have you heard if our moms made any plans for tomorrow?"

"No."

"I'll text my mom right now and see."

**Dakota:** Hey Mom, we're heading home. Do you and Mrs. Hansley have any plans for us tomorrow?

**Abigail:** We decided tomorrow would be a chill day after all the travel today. I'd like to go to the farmer's market in the morning and pick up some groceries, and then we'll probably just hang out at the apartment and relax.

Dakota read the message to Afton. "Do *you* have any plans for tomorrow, Afton?"

She tucked a strand of her light brown hair behind her ear. "Being with you?"

"Oh yeah?"

"Yeah."

"Like a daylong date?" Dakota asked.

"A daylong date would be amazing."

"Well, cool! I get that my mom just wants to chill for the day, but we might not be here long. So, I'd love to see more of the city if you're up for it, Afton."

"Let's! I'll be your personal tour guide."

"I bet you're the best tour guide."

"I don't know about that."

"Well, you're the cutest tour guide. I *do* know that!"

"You're too sweet, Dakota. Thank you. What would an all-day dream date in London look like to you?"

"Hmm, well, I think it would include a big breakfast, maybe a bike ride through one of those beautiful parks you mentioned, seeing some of the famous stuff—Big Ben, Westminster Abbey, Buckingham Palace—a delicious lunch maybe overlooking the River Thames, maybe a stop at the Sherlock Holmes Museum, a visit to the National Gallery, then a nice dinner somewhere."

Afton laughed. "Is that all?"

"Well, maybe after dinner, we could go to a play or watch a movie."

Afton looked at him in disbelief. "When did you fall out of Heaven, Dakota Knox? That sounds like the best day ever with the best guy ever."

"Well, let's do it!" Dakota said. "Let's have the best day ever."

"Let's!"

When they arrived at Afton's house, Dakota opened the glossy black door close to the sidewalk and walked with her through the lobby and onto the elevator. "What floor?"

"Third, please."

At her door, Afton reached into a pocket for her key fob. "It's been a delightful evening, Dakota. Thank you."

They hugged.

"Thank *you*, Afton. It's been a great day, for sure. Sleep well."

"You too. Text me when you wake up, and we'll begin our best day ever."

"Will do. Sweet dreams."

Before Dakota turned out the light that night, he opened his prayer journal and wrote: *Thank you, God, for Afton! What a special girl she is. You know that I love her. Would it bless You if we were boyfriend and girlfriend? Could we glorify You better if we were together in that kind of relationship? Could we strengthen and encourage one another better together or apart? Guide us, God.*

*One of the reasons I've held off on having a girlfriend is I've just never really known a girl that I felt was a good match for marriage. And I don't want to date just to date. The heartache and drama that comes with that . . . no thanks. But Afton, wow, God! She is someone I think I could marry and spend the rest of my life with. Might that be Your will for us?*

*Help me to be so careful with her heart. I don't want to hurt her in the slightest if things don't work out between us. I want to honor her as Your child, a daughter of the King! She is the most precious, beautiful person I've ever known. If we're not meant to be together, bless her with a wonderful godly guy. I love You, God! Amen.*

# Chapter 8

While Dakota and Afton enjoyed their apple crumble, Ahmed was at his laptop computer, placing an order for more ammo for Radomir's drone. Across from him at the dining table, Eeman and Avner were playing checkers.

"Missing your parents yet, Avner?" Eeman asked.

"Not yet."

"Your move. I'm sure they miss you."

"Yeah, don't remind me of that."

"They probably put missing-person signs all over Jerusalem. I can hear the headlines in the news: 'Museum director's son vanishes—parents heartbroken.'"

"Stop!"

"Sorry, dude. Crown me."

"I'm done." Avner flipped the checkerboard over and walked off toward his new living quarters at the western end of Radomir's mansion.

A Rottweiler that Sabiya was petting at a nearby couch, jumped to its feet and started barking.

"Whoa—Avner's mad," Eeman said.

"You're foolish for bringing up his parents," Ahmed said. "He just got here, and Radomir already yelled at him earlier."

"So wait," Sabiya said. "Avner helped you guys with the heist in Jerusalem?"

"Yeah," Ahmed said. "He worked at the museum, and Radomir paid him for his help. But the police were on to him, so we snuck him out of the country."

"And he's going to work for Radomir, here on the estate?"

Sabiya asked.

Ahmed struck a match to light the cigarette hanging from his lips. "Yep. Radomir offered him a job."

"Ahmed, were you able to trace the van's license plate yet?" Eeman asked.

"I'm going to work on that right now."

A few minutes later, Ahmed pointed at his computer screen. "There it is! A white Mercedes passenger van. It's registered to the London Marriott Hotel at Grosvenor Square. That must be where Dakota Knox is staying."

"That twerp thinks he's so smart following us to England," Eeman said. "He doesn't know who he's messing with."

Sabiya closed her magazine and stood. "What are you guys going to do?"

"It's best you don't know, sis."

Sabiya yawned. "All right, boys. I'm going to bed. Goodnight."

After she left the room, Eeman cleaned up the checkers. "So, what's the plan, Ahmed?"

"We'll go scout out the Marriott tomorrow, maybe sit in the lobby for a couple of hours, keep an eye on the door. If management hassles us, we'll reserve some rooms with views of the exit. We'll find him."

"Sounds good," Eeman said. "He's dead meat!"

# Chapter 9
## Wednesday, June 22, Marylebone, London.

Dakota woke up early the following day. He smiled when he remembered that he and Afton were on the verge of having their "best day ever." He had enough experience though to know that things don't always go according to plan. So, he prayed.

*Good morning, Lord. I love You! Thank You for a new day and good health to go out and enjoy it. The day is Yours. Afton and I have our plans, but we belong to You. So, modify them according to Your will. May we magnify and bless You in all that we do. Amen.*

He unplugged his phone and messaged Afton:

**Dakota:** Hey Afton. Good morning. I'm up. You?

**Afton:** Yes. Been up for a while. Still on Israel's time.

**Dakota:** I'm excited to spend the day with you. Best day ever straight ahead.

**Afton:** Yes! So excited. I mapped out some things for us to do, starting with breakfast.

**Dakota:** Awesome. I can come over whenever you're ready.

**Afton:** Sounds good. How about twenty minutes?

**Dakota:** Perfect.

**Afton:** The weather forecast is pretty warm during the day. But the evening is going to be chilly. Unless we're coming back here to change, I'm thinking we should pack some warmer clothes in a backpack.

**Dakota:** That sounds good. I'll bring my backpack.

**Afton:** Great. See you soon.

On his way over to Afton's, Dakota walked across the quiet street to Bryanston Square Park. He pulled out his "tactical" wallet he purchased from a company called Dango. The metal and leather wallet had a heat-treated, corrosion-resistant stainless steel multi-tool in it as thin as his ATM card. In a pinch, the tool could be used to saw, cut, pry nails, tighten nuts and bolts, and, more importantly, open a cold bottle of Virgil's root beer, his favorite soda. He slid the tool halfway out of the wallet, locked it into place, and cut off a beautiful white rose.

*Wow. That smells amazing. Afton will love this.*

He took the elevator up to the Hansley's flat.

She opened the door. "Good morning."

"Good morning. This is for you."

"What a pretty rose. Thank you, Dakota. That's so sweet of you."

"You're welcome."

"I'm going to bring it with us."

"You ready to have the best day ever?" Dakota asked.

"For sure. Let's go." She turned around before walking out.

"Bye Mom! I'll be back tonight."

"Have fun, you two. Be careful," Mrs. Hansley said.

"Always!" Afton said as she shut the door. She looked at Dakota and said, "Hey, we're sort of twinning."

Afton was wearing a white tee shirt, cut-off blue denim shorts, white tennis shoes, and a light blue logo-less ball cap.

Dakota had on a white tee shirt, a pair of light blue shorts, beige sneakers, and his brown and yellow Padres cap.

Afton said, "Can I throw these clothes in your backpack?"

"Of course."

As the elevator descended to the ground floor, Afton said, "You hungry?"

"For sure."

"Good!"

They walked about three blocks to one of Afton's favorite places for breakfast.

"I'll take a veggie omelet," Afton told the waitress, "and a vanilla latte."

"I'll have an Americano-black," Dakota said, "two eggs, scrambled, two slices of bacon, a side of fruit, and a stack of four pancakes."

"Would you like the fluffy American kind?" the waitress asked.

"Is there another kind?" Dakota asked.

"Yes, English pancakes. They're thin like crepes."

"Oh. Those don't sound very filling. I'll take the American style then. Thank you."

"You got it," the waitress said. "And I love your accent. Let me guess—California?"

"Uh, yeah," Dakota said, surprised by her accuracy.

N

Regent's Park ●

Sherlock Holmes Museum ●

MARYLEBONE

Hansleys' Home ●
Knoxes' Rental House ●

Marriott Hotel ●

LONDON

British Museum ●

Covent Garden Station ●

Embankment Pier ●

Victoria Embankment Park ●

St. James's Park ●

Buckingham Palace ●

Big Ben ●

Westminster Abbey ●

BLOOMSBURY

SOHO

PICCADILLY

"And I'd even be so bold as to narrow it down to Southern California."

"You're good," Dakota said.

"And I'd even say you sound like you're from San Diego."

"Wow."

As the waitress walked away, Dakota said, "She knows accents really well."

Afton smiled. "And baseball teams."

"What do you mean?"

"Your Padres hat, silly. She was playing with you. You have a San Diego Padres hat on. *That's* how she knew where you're from."

"Oops. I forgot."

"But you *do* have an accent," Afton said, "and I think it's adorable!"

• • •

As Dakota and Afton enjoyed their breakfast, a black Audi A8 sedan backed into a parking spot across the street from the Marriott hotel at Grosvenor Square.

Eeman turned off the engine.

"Here's the plan," Ahmed said. We'll head inside and sit in the lobby. I want you to keep an eye on the main entrance. I'm going to sit closer to the elevator and watch for Dakota there. He's got to come through the lobby eventually. When we spot him, we'll follow him outside or onto the elevator and take him out."

"And the girl too, right?" Eeman asked.

"Right, if they're together. Dakota's our primary target. If we get the girl, that's a bonus. But we need to knock them off in a place where we can do it cleanly—not in the hotel lobby where there's a bunch of cameras."

"Got it!"

"Follow my lead."

"Dakota's so dumb. Did he really think he'd be able to come to London and track down the other artifacts? Stupid!"

"Your gun's ready?" Ahmed asked.

"Yep. Yours?"

"Of course. Let's head in."

The two men walked into the 5-star luxury hotel and sat down in the lobby.

• • •

After breakfast, Afton said, "You ready for our second stop?"

"Sure. Where are you taking me, tour guide?"

"Well, I mapped out the things you said would make up a dream date in London so that we could pull off as much as possible in one day."

"We don't have to do all of it," Dakota said. "It was sort of a crazy list. Maybe we just take our time, and we can do the other stuff another day."

"That sounds good."

"So, where's the next stop?"

"The Sherlock Holmes Museum. It's only a couple of blocks away. Follow me and hold my hand. I don't want you getting lost."

"Gladly, Miss Hansley."

A few minutes later, Dakota said, "I see the Sherlock

Holmes statue up ahead. That must be it, the famous house at 221B Baker Street."

"That's it."

Dakota bought their tickets, and they headed in through a black door. They walked up the narrow staircase to the first floor. "It feels like we've stepped back in time about a hundred years, doesn't it?"

"It does," Afton said.

At the top of the stairs, they were welcomed by a butler who told them about Sherlock Holmes and ushered them into Holmes's office. It was perfectly preserved, as described in the fictional stories Dakota had read as a kid.

As they wandered through the four-story house, Dakota briefly explained the significance of a random violin, a chemistry set, some wax figures from Sherlock Holmes's most famous cases, and why the letters VR had been shot into the wall. On their way out, they walked through the gift shop.

"Hank loves the Sherlock Holmes books. Maybe I'll buy him a little something."

Dakota found a small compass with a keychain. "He'll like this."

"I think so," Afton said.

Dakota paid the cashier and slid the compass into his backpack. They walked outside. "Thanks, Afton. I enjoyed that. Where should we go next?"

"Well, you mentioned riding bikes and riding around one of the pretty parks we have. So, follow me. There's a bike rental place a couple of blocks away. We can pick up bikes there and leave them at any of their drop-off locations around London when we're done."

"Awesome, Miss Hansley. Hold my hand. Don't lose me."

"Yes, sir, I'd hate to lose you, Mr. Knox."

When they arrived at the bikes, Afton placed her white rose in a basket on the handlebars. With an app on her phone, she paid for and unlocked the bikes. They pedaled off, and Afton said, "**Regent's Park** is right across this street. I think you'll like it. Follow me."

As they rode into the south end of the park, Afton said, "Let's go to the right. This paved road we're on goes around the outer perimeter of the park. It's about a three-mile loop. But there is a left up here that leads to the park's interior where there are rose gardens, a lake, fountains, statues—it's lovely. This land used to be a hunting ground for King Henry, the eighth, back in the fifteen hundreds."

"That's cool. I love all the trees everywhere."

"So do I."

They found a bike rack, locked the bikes, and walked along a path through Queen Mary's Rose Garden. As they neared

Boating Lake, a young lady with red hair jogged toward them. Afton said, "That's my friend, Kylie, running toward us. I haven't seen her for a while."

Kylie stopped when she recognized Afton. "Hey, Afton!"

"Hi, Kylie! It's so good to see you. This is my friend Dakota."

"It's a pleasure to meet you, Dakota. I thought you were in Israel for the summer, Afton."

"I was. It's a long story, but I may be going back in a week or two. How are you doing, Kylie?"

"Really good."

"Well, I know they miss you in the high school youth group. You're always welcome back. We all miss you and love you."

"Thanks, I'm pretty done with religion. Sort of doing my own thing now. But I'm glad it makes other people happy." She looked at her watch. "I don't want my heart rate to go down too much; I should keep running. So nice to bump into you guys."

After she ran off, Afton said, "Kylie stopped going to our high school group about six months ago."

"Do you know why?"

"Well, I asked her, and she said her new boyfriend had convinced her that the New Testament authors borrowed major details for Jesus's life from earlier sources, other religions, that were around *before* the rise of Christianity."

"In other words," Dakota said, "they plagiarized Jesus's life story."

"Yes, she said that. I asked her for an example, and she said . . . let me find her text. She said:

**Kylie:** Horus, one of the gods worshipped in ancient

Egypt, was born to a virgin on December 25, worshipped by three kings. He was a teacher by age twelve. He had twelve disciples. He was called "The Lamb of God," crucified, buried for three days, and then resurrected. Sound familiar? Jesus was a clever invention by deceitful men 2,000 years ago.

"Ah yes," Dakota said. "It sounds like Kylie and her boyfriend watched *Zeitgeist*."

"A movie?"

"It's a low-budget video that went viral on social media a while back, but it's still out there on YouTube. It popularized this Horus-plagiarism garbage."

"Oh, wow."

"Some students in our youth group were really questioning their faith after watching the video. So our youth pastor brought in a professor of world religions—he's authored several books on ancient religions—and he addressed the claims in the *Zeitgeist* video. His presentation was super interesting."

"What did you learn about it?" Afton asked.

"Basically, that everything your friend told you about Horus is *false* . . . provably false."

"Really! Let's keep walking but go on."

"Well," Dakota said, "Horus was a *mythological* deity, not a real historical person like Jesus. So, it's hard to even compare the two. It would be like discounting news reports about the International Space Station because there were some similarities between it and the *Star Trek* television show that preceded it."

"That would be dumb."

"The professor said every encyclopedia and dictionary on ancient religions says that Horus *wasn't* born to a virgin. The ancient myths say that he was conceived by his parents, Isis and Osiris. And nowhere do the myths say Horus was born on December 25. And even if he had been, the Bible doesn't even say what day Jesus was born on."

"Good point," Afton said.

"The December twenty-fifth tradition originated long after the Gospels were written. And the Gospel accounts of Jesus's birth don't mention three kings, only magi—commonly known as wise men, not kings.

"And Horus was never crucified. Crucifixion had not even been invented at the time *Zeitgeist* says the Horus myth originated around three thousand BC. Horus is not even reported to have died in most Egyptian myths. So, needless to say, Horus was never resurrected.

"And the myths don't say anything about Horus becoming a teacher at age twelve or having twelve disciples."

"So, it sounds like the *Zeitgeist* video is brimming with misinformation," Afton said.

"For sure. I know of articles online that refute the claims in **Zeitgeist**. Maybe Kylie would be willing to read one of them."

"Maybe! Send me the links when you're able."

About twenty minutes later, the two teens hopped back on their bikes.

"This is a great park, Afton. I love it. Where are we off to next?"

"Well, Mr. Knox, let's finish riding the loop around the park, and then our next stop will be Buckingham Palace."

With the best British accent he could muster, Dakota asked, "Might we see the royal family and be invited in for tea?"

"Cute, Dakota. Probably not, but I *do* have tickets for a tour."

As they pedaled south towards Buckingham Palace, Dakota noticed that his back tire was low on air.

"Hey, Afton, I must have a leak in my tire. Do you know if there's a bike station nearby where I could exchange the bike?"

"Let's pull over, and I'll check the app."

They stopped under the canopy of a tall tree. Dakota pulled out his water bottle from his backpack and took a swig. "Ice water tastes so good on a warm day. You thirsty, Afton? I have your water bottle in my backpack."

"I'm good, thanks. It looks like the next bike station is a ways off. But I have an idea. The hotel my uncle Chad manages is three blocks away. I bet he has a pump in his car. He rides a bike quite often. Let's go check."

# Chapter 10

Dakota and Afton pedaled their bikes and stopped near the entrance of the **Marriott Hotel at Grosvenor Square**.

"I'll message my uncle and see if he's working today."

"If he's not," Dakota said, "There might be enough air in the tire to make it to the next bike station."

"Okay, we'll see."

A couple of minutes later, Afton's uncle texted back. She read the text and told Dakota, "He's not here. He works later tonight."

• • •

Eeman had grown bored with keeping an eye on the hotel's front door. He was slumped in a chair with his feet up, engaged in a video game on his phone. He briefly looked up at the door when the game ended, then back down.

It took a few seconds for his mind to process what he saw. He looked up a second time. Through the glass door, he saw *the girl*. She was just starting to pedal away.

He jumped to his feet. "Ahmed! Let's go."

Ahmed hurried over. "What'd you see?"

"The girl. I swear, it was her! She's outside on a bike."

Ahmed and Eeman rushed outside and looked in both directions.

"There they are! They went left," Eeman said. "That's Dakota and the girl on the bikes."

Ahmed said, "They're too far away to catch by foot. Let's get the car. We'll find them."

The two men scrambled around the corner of the hotel and jumped into the black Audi.

"How'd they get past us?" Ahmed yelled.

"Maybe there's another exit."

Eeman peeled out of the parking space and turned down the street.

• • •

When Afton found out her uncle wasn't working, she and Dakota decided to pedal to the closest bike station. Dakota's back tire was mushy, having lost about half of its air, but he managed to keep moving, though slower than usual.

Afton was looking at the map on the bike-rental app. "You know what? We're going in the wrong direction. Let's cut through this alley and backtrack a bit. Sorry, Dakota."

"It's all good. We're not in a hurry."

When they arrived at the bike station, they docked Dakota's bike in the rack and checked out another one. After a high five, they rode their bikes toward Buckingham Palace.

"Afton, we're doing all the things *I* mentioned for a dream date. What would *your* dream date be?"

She looked at him and smiled. "I'm living it right now."

Dakota was blessed knowing Afton was having a good time.

They parked and locked the bikes near Buckingham Palace.

"Oh, we have to hurry," Afton said. "The tour I got tickets for starts in a couple of minutes. There's the queue."

"The Q?"

"The line of people. Brits call lines of people *queues*."

"Didn't know that!"

"We're learning all kinds of interesting things today, aren't we?"

"We are."

They hurried through the crowds of people and stood at the back of the line.

• • •

The **Audi** came to a screeching stop at a red light.

Ahmed pointed to the right. "Dakota and the girl rode by this direction. Go, go!"

"You think they're going to Buckingham Palace?"

"I don't know, but that's the direction I saw them ride by."

"But if they're here to track down the artifacts," Eeman said, "why would they go to Buckingham Palace? Maybe they're enlisting the King's help."

"There they are!" Ahmed said, "Like a hundred meters away, crossing the street. They're on their feet. Park the car!"

"I can't park here!" Eeman yelled.

"We need to get out. Park it!"

Eeman abruptly turned the car into the curb and brought

the car to a sudden stop with two wheels up on the sidewalk.

Ahmed shook his head. "Who taught you how to park? Is this how they drive in Iraq? Turn on the hazard lights, and let's go. Hopefully, the car will be here when we come back."

The two men ran toward the crowd of people gathered outside the palace.

"They're right there in that line," Eeman said.

But it was too late. Dakota and Afton's tour group was invited in, and the door was shut.

"I'll buy tickets on my phone," Ahmed said, "and we'll go in with the next group."

Eeman looked surprised. "We're going to shoot them inside **Buckingham Palace**?"

"No, there are metal detectors at the entrance. Give me your gun. We'll hide our guns here in this bush. I have something else I can use." He tapped on a pocket in his jeans.

• • •

As the two teens walked into the palace, Afton said, "I read that there are 775 rooms in Buckingham Palace."

"Whoa. That's crazy."

"So, this is a self-guided tour. We can stay thirty minutes or up to two hours."

They held hands and walked through the beautifully decorated State Rooms, past the magnificent Grand Staircase, and admired paintings by Rembrandt, Canaletto, and Vermeer.

"So the King lives here?" Dakota asked.

"Yes, but he has other homes around the country. He's not here at Buckingham currently."

• • •

Ahmed and Eeman walked into the palace thirty minutes after Dakota and Afton's group.

"Wow. I didn't know you have diabetes and take insulin shots every day," Eeman said.

"I don't."

"But you told the security guard when he asked about your syringe—"

"Just be quiet and listen. We're going to find Dakota and the girl. Then you're going to distract the girl. Easy. Got it?"

"Got it. Distract the girl."

"Then I'm going to come up behind Dakota and jab him with this syringe. He'll appear to faint a few seconds later. We'll calmly walk off, and he'll be dead in two or three minutes."

"Whoa, I didn't know insulin could do that to people. Why doesn't it kill you?"

"Because it's not insulin, and I don't inject it into my body."

"Then how do you stay alive if you have diabetes?"

"I'm *not* a diabetic," Ahmed whispered. "But you know what I *am*? Exasperated."

"Is that a different disease? Or, no, that's like being constipated? There's probably a restroom somewhere."

Ahmed turned away, shaking his head. "*Why*? Why is he Radomir's bodyguard?"

• • •

Dakota was looking at some of the royal jewelry in a display case. "You know, Afton, I think I've seen enough. What about you?"

"I'm good."

"This place is cool," Dakota said, "but how much gold does one need to see in a day? The streets of Heaven are going to be made of gold."

"Right," Afton said. "Why don't we head out?"

"Lead the way, Miss Hansley. I forget where the exit is."

"Actually, when I was here on a school field trip, there was a side door exit over this way. Maybe it's still there."

They turned a corner and walked down a hall.

"There's the door," Afton said.

As they walked out, Dakota heard someone yell, "Hey, stop!"

Dakota looked at Afton. "Maybe we weren't supposed to go out that door."

"Maybe not. I don't know. Let's not wait around to find out. Come on!"

They started jogging back to the bikes.

Dakota said, "I didn't see a sign on the door that said, 'Not an exit.' Did you?"

"No."

When they got to the bikes, they saw two men running toward them.

"Oh, boy," Dakota said. "Two plain-clothed security officers. Let's go!"

Dakota and Afton hopped on the bikes and quickly pedaled off. A few blocks down the street, Afton said, "They should mark their doors better."

"Well, forget about it," Dakota said. "I'm sure we're not the first people to go out a wrong door."

"Right, and it's not like we stole anything."

"Why don't we get lunch somewhere?"

"I'm hungry. What do you feel like, Mr. Knox?"

"You like Indian food. I like Indian food. What about that place over there?"

"Let's do it."

As they walked into the restaurant, Afton said, "Brits love fish and chips, but Indian food is probably the most loved dish. Chicken tikka masala is actually a British dish."

"I didn't know that. Well, *that's* what I'll order then."

"Why don't we get it to go and eat outside at Saint James's Park? It's a beautiful setting."

"Love that idea! You're the best tour guide, Miss Hansley."

"You're pretty easy, Mr. Knox."

When their food was ready, they made the short ride to the park and found a couple of empty deckchairs underneath a tree overlooking **Saint James's Park Lake**.

"This food smells delicious. Why don't I pray for us?"

Dakota said.

"Please."

"Dear God, thank You for this amazing day and this beautiful setting. We are so blessed. Thank You for this food. Bless it to our bodies, and it's in Jesus's name we pray. Amen."

"Amen." As they enjoyed their Indian food, Afton said, "See those pelicans over there?"

"Yeah."

"They've lived in St. James's Park for nearly four hundred years. They were a gift from a Russian ambassador to King Charles, the second."

"I didn't know pelicans could live four hundred years."

"No. I meant—"

"I'm just messin' with you. That's cool. Afton, I have a fun question for you. If you could go anywhere in the world for a week, all expenses paid, where would it be?"

"That *is* a fun question." She thought about it for a few

seconds. "Tahiti."

"Really!"

"Yep, hiking through tropical forests, swimming in clear warm ocean water, and walking along the shorelines on white sandy beaches sounds amazing."

"That *does* sound amazing," Dakota said.

"What about you? Where would you go?"

"Costa Rica."

"Ooh, that's interesting. Why?"

"It seems like a beautiful place. It's close to the equator, so the water is warm. There's great surf there. There are tropical jungles to explore, monkeys, iguanas, toucans, volcanos—it just seems like a really cool place to visit."

When they finished eating, Afton said, "Are you ready for our next stop, Mr. Knox?"

"I am. Where to?"

"Westminster Abbey."

# Chapter 11

"Westminster Abbey is just a short walk over this way," Afton said, "so we can leave the bikes locked up. Follow me, Dakota. And remember to hold my hand, please."

"You got it, Miss Hansley."

They stopped at a crosswalk and waited for the walk signal. When it lit up, Afton stepped into the road, and Dakota yanked her back. A tow truck was coming from the right fast enough for Dakota to realize the driver was going to run the red light. And he did.

"Whoa, bro! Pay attention," Dakota yelled.

"Thanks for pulling me back. That was crazy."

"You're welcome. I'm glad you're all right."

"Yeah, I'm fine. Let's go."

"I tried to see the license plate number, maybe to call it in and report him, but it was towing a black Audi that blocked the view."

A couple of minutes later, Afton said, "So, **Westminster Abbey** is a famous church, as you know. It's more than seven hundred years old. Several British kings and queens and some well-known Christians are buried here."

"I know Isaac Newton is buried here."

"Yes! One of the most influential scientists of all time."

"What other famous Christians?"

"A couple that come to mind are George Handel, one of Britain's greatest composers, and David Livingstone, the explorer, and missionary to Africa."

The two teens walked through the church, looking at the

gothic architecture and high ceilings.

Dakota strolled over to a marble statue of a man sitting in a chair. He read the name: William Wilberforce. "He's buried here too? Wow."

"Remind me who he was."

"We learned about him in my church history class my junior year. Wilberforce was a Christian and a member of the

British Parliament in the late seventeen hundreds. He spent twenty-plus years fighting for the abolition of slavery. And his efforts finally paid off. The U.K. abolished the slave trade in the British Empire in 1807."

"That's cool, Dakota. This is where he's buried!"

"I look forward to meeting him in Heaven."

"Look who's buried over this way. Charles Darwin."

"Wow," Dakota said, shaking his head. "His theory of evolution has misled millions of people to abandon belief in a creator. Sad."

"There are so many problems with the theory," Afton said.

"Absolutely," Dakota said as they continued walking. "One fatal blow is the fossil record. If evolution really is the explanation for all of life, the fossil record should show continuous and gradual changes from the bottom layer to the top layers. But it doesn't. Nearly all groups of animals appear in the fossil record suddenly, simultaneously, fully developed, and with absolutely no hint that they evolved from anything else. Those facts are devastating to the theory of human **evolution**."

"For sure," Afton said. "The fossil record is evidence for a global flood, not evolution."

"Totally."

They looked around a little longer.

"Where might we be headed next?"

"I'm glad you asked, Mr. Knox."

"Follow me. Big Ben is a close walk."

On their way, Dakota spotted an ice-cream vendor with a sidewalk cart. "Miss Hansley, may I interest you in an ice cream on this warm summer day?"

"Why, yes, you may."

"What kind would you like?"

"How about that Dark Chocolate Raspberry Bar."

"That sounds good. Hank told me that I had to try one of these 'Magnum Infinity Chocolate' bars."

Ice creams in hand, they walked around the corner and looked up at the iconic clock.

"So, that's **Big Ben**," Afton said. "Why don't we cross the bridge and look at it from the other side of the river? That will be a better view."

On the south side of the River Thames, Afton pointed at the large neo-gothic building. "That's where the U.K. Parliament meets. And that clock is Big Ben. Well, technically, Big Ben is the name of the massive bell inside the tower. It weighs more than thirteen tons!"

"That's big! How often does it ring?"

"At the top of every hour. And other bells every fifteen minutes."

"I've seen pictures of it for years. How cool to see it in person. Thanks, Afton."

"Of course. Let's walk back to Saint James's Park and get the bikes."

As they walked across the bridge, Afton said, "You mentioned the National Gallery yesterday when you were describing our dream date. Would you like to go there next? It's not far from here. If not, I have another idea."

"I kind of feel like I saw enough paintings at Buckingham Palace. What's your idea?"

"Well, I thought it might be more fun if we turn the bikes in and hop on a double-decker bus and ride around the city. You'll see a ton, and then we can get off whenever and get dinner somewhere."

"Miss Hansley! That sounds like a brilliant idea."

$$\bullet\ \bullet\ \bullet$$

As Dakota and Afton headed back to Saint James's Park, Eeman and Ahmed walked away from Buckingham Palace. Ahmed kicked a trash can by the side of the road. "I can't believe we don't have a car!"

"I can," Eeman said. "You told me to pull the car over there. It was clearly marked, 'No parking.'"

"I know—stop! We have to figure out where it got towed and how to get it back. Let's go back to the Marriott. I'll get us a couple of rooms and work on it. And you can keep an eye out for Dakota. Although, he and the girl might already be back at the hotel. Maybe we can pay a bellhop or maid to spill the beans."

"Spill the beans?"

"Uh, tell us if they've seen Dakota," Ahmed said.

"But why would we pay them to make a mess with beans? Oh, like if the beans are spread on the floor in the lobby, and it's slippery, maybe Dakota will slip on them, and then we grab him?"

"Are you serious?"

"Yeah."

"You're about as sharp as a bowling ball, aren't you?"

"Um . . . I don't bowl. I don't get it."

"Of course you don't."

"Hey, Ahmed, we're not going to *walk* all the way to the hotel, are we? It's pretty far. Let's just catch a **bus** headed for Grosvenor Square."

• • •

Dakota and Afton docked the bikes and walked to a nearby bus stop. When the bus pulled up to the curb, Dakota motioned with his hand. "After you, Miss Hansley."

"Would you like to sit up top, Mr. Knox? You'll be able to see more."

"Sure."

They found two empty seats near the back on the right side.

"You take the window seat, Dakota."

"Thank you."

A couple of minutes later, the bus stopped at the curb. As the new passengers were finding their seats, Dakota did a double-take. He lowered his voice and said, "Don't look now, but those two plain-clothed officers that work at Buckingham Palace just boarded the bus. That's them standing near the front."

"They must be on their way home from work," Afton said.

"Yeah, I don't think they'll arrest us or anything."

"All we did was walk out the wrong door. They see thousands of people every day. They won't recognize us."

"Let's take our hats off, just in case," Dakota said. "Here, we can put them in my backpack."

"Why don't we get off the bus at the next stop in Mayfair just to be safe?" Afton said. "And we'll catch the next bus."

"That sounds good."

When the bus came to a stop, Dakota and Afton stood. As Dakota put his backpack on, he noticed that the two men were walking toward them.

"Afton! Turn around. They're getting off here."

Afton turned her back to the men and stepped sideways out of the aisle. Dakota looked down and turned his face away.

The taller of the two men with broad shoulders and black curly hair brushed against Afton's shoulder.

"Excuse me," he said.

A couple of seconds later, the men descended the stairs at the back of the bus and walked off.

Afton and Dakota sat back down.

"Phew! That was close, Dakota."

"Not that we were in trouble or anything, but still."

"Okay, we'll stay on and enjoy the ride."

• • •

Eeman and Ahmed walked from the bus stop to the **Marriott**. Ahmed approached a bellhop, pulled out a 50-pound note, and handed it to the young man. "Hey, this is for you. We're staying here at the hotel, and we're supposed to meet a coworker here today. Might you be able to look on the hotel computer and let us know if a Dakota Knox has arrived?"

"Unfortunately, I can't do that, sir."

Ahmed handed him another 50-pound note. "Surely, you can help us for a—"

"I can't, sir. I'm sorry. Maybe you could call your coworker."

Eeman pulled the 50-pound notes out of the man's hand. "We're taking these back then."

The two men headed inside. Ahmed went to the front desk to reserve a couple of rooms overlooking the hotel's entrance.

The woman behind the counter said, "I only have one room available with a view of the front of the hotel. It has two twin beds. Might that work?"

"I guess. Yes."

While the woman made their keys, Eeman asked, "Do you guys sell beans in the snack shop?"

"Jelly beans? Yes."

"No, like the slippery beans. The wet kind."

She looked at him with a confused look on her face. "No, I don't believe so."

Eeman whispered to Ahmed, "Scratch that idea."

The men walked to the elevator. Ahmed pushed the up button. "I hate sharing a room with you, Eeman. You snore like a freaking monster. I can hardly sleep. People *next door* can't sleep. They call the front desk and say, 'Help! We think there's a grizzly bear in the hallway!'"

"That only happened once. Jam some tissue in your ears."

"Oh, I'm going to."

"So, what's the plan, Ahmed?"

"I'm going to figure out where Radomir's car got towed."

"I mean with Dakota and the girl."

Ahmed opened the door to the hotel room on the fourth floor. He walked to the window and looked out over Duke Street and the hotel entrance. "This is perfect. So, here's the plan. Pull up a chair here and keep an eye on the activity coming and going from the entrance. If you see them and have a clear shot, take them out. Then we slide out of here, disappear into the confusion, and walk away."

"They have your ID and credit card info at the front desk. If they trace the gunshots back to this room, they'll—"

"Really, Eeman?"

"Oh, right. I forgot. The ID and credit card are bogus."

"Totally bogus."

Eeman opened the window, sat in a gray chair, and set his

gun on a nearby end table.

An hour later, Ahmed's phone rang. It was Radomir.

"Hey, what's up, Boss?"

"Did you kill the boy?"

"Not yet. We know where he's staying, and we're staking out the hotel entrance, waiting to get a shot."

"Good. On a sad note, Avner is no longer with us."

"He left?"

"No, he's dead."

"Oh. What happened?"

"Dagon and Titan attacked him this morning. I was in the front yard and heard screaming coming out of my office. Apparently, Avner walked in there. Why he would go in there, I don't know. But the dogs ripped him to shreds. It was a bloody mess . . . really gross."

"Wow. Is his body still in your office?"

"No. Dario and I carried it to the backyard and covered it with a tarp. Sabiya cleaned up the blood . . . She's pretty shaken up."

"I can imagine. Okay."

"I'd like for Eeman to bury him when you guys get home. I'm thinking next to the guy that worked at the Pergamon Museum."

"Okay, Boss. I'll tell him," Ahmed said.

"And I trust you'll find time today to go into Avner's bitcoin account and transfer the funds I paid him back to me."

"I'll do that."

"Keep me up to date on Dakota and the girl."

"Will do."

Radomir ended the call.

# Chapter 12
## Wednesday, June 22, London.

Afton pointed out friends' homes and other landmarks to Dakota as the double-decker bus went up and down London's streets.

"It's getting close to dinner time, Dakota. What kind of food are you in the mood for?"

"I'd love to take you to a really nice place."

"You would?"

"Yeah. I found it online last night. It's in a building called **'The Shard.'** It's like eighty-two stories tall. Have you heard of it?"

"I have. It's pretty well known here in London, you sweet guy."

"I read that it's Western Europe's tallest building and has 360-degree views of London. May I take you to dinner there?"

"Of course, Dakota. That's very nice of you. I've heard there are some amazing restaurants at The Shard. They're pretty expensive, though. Are you sure?"

"I'm sure."

"Okay. Fun! Which one were you thinking?"

"I thought Oblix's menu looked good. It's on the thirty-second floor."

"Let's go!"

They got off the bus at the next stop. Dakota made a reservation on his phone, and Afton waved down a cab.

When they arrived at The Shard on the south side of the River Thames, they went through security, found the restrooms, and changed into the clothes Dakota had in his backpack.

"I'm so glad we packed our jeans and sweaters," Afton said.

"So am I. I love your white sweater—is that wool?"

"Oh, thanks, yes. I love how soft and warm it is."

"Well, let's head up. Our reservation is in five minutes."

The hostess sat them at a candle-lit table by a window.

"Wow," Dakota said. "What a view of the city and the river!"

"It's beautiful."

When the waiter came, Afton ordered the seabass with lemon hollandaise, creamed spinach with Parmesan, and a salad. Dakota ordered a steak with creamy peppercorn sauce, a salad, and baked gratin potatoes with garlic and rosemary.

When they were done with dinner, Dakota reached his right hand across the table and held Afton's. "Miss Hansley, the last few weeks have been the best days of my life. Meeting you in Herzliya, getting to know you, exploring Israel with you, surfing with you, enjoying meals with you. It's all been so . . . wonderful . . . Afton Hansley, I *love* you! And I . . . well . . . I'd like to know if you'll be my girlfriend?"

Afton smiled at Dakota with the happiest smile. She nodded her head. "Yes! I'd love to be your girlfriend. Dakota, you are the sweetest, most fun, godly, smart, handsome guy I've ever known. I love you too!"

"Really. Wow. I'm so glad. I texted your dad in Israel this morning and asked for his permission for us to date, and he said *yes*."

"You did?"

"Yeah, is that a problem?"

"Not at all. Just . . . I don't hear of or know of any guys that do that anymore. I think that's amazing, and I'm sure my dad

The Shard

River Thames

Tower Bridge

was happy about it."

"Well, it was important for me to have his approval."

"How could he object, Dakota? He thinks you're great."

"Well, I think he's great too. I know we already had ice cream this afternoon, but I think we should celebrate with dessert."

"Why don't we share something? What looks good to you?"

"This toffee banana and crème brûlée tart with coffee ice cream sounds amazing."

When they finished dessert, Dakota said, "Why don't we go up to the observation deck on the seventy-second floor before we head out?"

"I thought heights make you nervous. Remember the tram at Masada?"

"Well, yeah, I don't like gondolas and trams that are high up and hanging on cables, but tall buildings aren't a problem."

"Okay. So you'll be fine?"

"Totally fine."

They took the high-speed elevator up to the seventy-second floor and walked out onto the open-air sky deck.

Afton pointed and said, "That bridge right there is called **'Tower Bridge.'** The bridge lifts in the middle to let large vessels through. That fortress-palace building next to it on the north side of the river is called 'The Tower of London.' It's nearly a thousand years old."

"Wow."

Dakota asked a nearby woman, "Would you mind taking a picture of us? And if you could get the Tower Bridge in the picture, that'd be amazing."

After she took a few photos, Afton said, "Let's walk over

here and look west. Hold my hand, *boyfriend*."

"Gladly, girlfriend."

"Look there. That massive building is Saint Paul's Cathedral. That Ferris-wheel thing is called 'The Eye'—it's the world's tallest observation wheel. Over there is Buckingham Palace where we got in trouble with the King, and there's Big Ben. . . . What a view, Dakota."

"I love it. We are so high up."

"And I love the fresh air, though it's a bit chilly."

"May I put my arm around you to keep you warm?"

"I'd like that."

He put his arm around her shoulder, and she put hers around his lower back. They meandered around, looking down on the city from different angles.

"The city looks so peaceful from up here . . . it's just lovely."

"*You're* lovely, Miss Hansley."

"I love you, Mr. Knox."

A few minutes later, they decided to head home.

"How far of a walk would it be back to Bryanston Square?" Dakota asked.

"About four miles."

"I thought we'd get a cab or take the Tube, but it's not that late. Would you be up for walking back?"

"Sure, under one condition," Afton said.

"What's that?"

"You hold my hand or keep your arm around me the whole way."

"Hmm . . . let me think about it. Okay, *if I must*."

As they walked across the bridge over the river, they talked about how blessed they were to connect in Israel.

Dakota explained to her that he had never had a girlfriend, except maybe once in third grade, but that only lasted a couple of weeks and ended when he wouldn't share the swing.

"Have you had a boyfriend, Afton?"

"Yeah, I have. One. We broke up about nine months ago."

"What happened, if you don't mind me asking?"

"It's fine. I shouldn't have gotten in a relationship with him. He wasn't a Christian. We only dated for about three months. And then he broke up with me."

"It's hard to believe that someone would break up with you. Was he out of his mind?"

"No. He wanted to take our relationship 'to the next level' physically, if you know what I mean. And I said, 'No. I'm not doing that. I'm a Christian, and I'm going to wait until I'm married.' And he couldn't understand that. Let me reword that. He understood what I said very well; he just wanted to do things *his* way, not God's. And so, he broke up with me."

"That's awesome of you for taking a stand like that, honoring God. But that was probably still a hard time for you?"

"Yeah, for a couple of weeks. But, you know Dakota, I thank God that he broke up with me. I shouldn't have been dating him. The Bible makes it clear that Christians should not be unequally yoked with nonbelievers."

"You're right."

"And as I've grown in my relationship with God, these past nine months, I've come to see how important it is to be with someone who, not just *claims* to be a Christian, but who proves by his life that he's a *solid* Christian and who truly *loves* the Lord."

"I agree. That's so important. Thanks for sharing all that

with me, Afton. Well, not having had a girlfriend, you may have already guessed that I'm a virgin. And I want to wait until I'm married too."

Afton smiled at Dakota. "That is so precious, Dakota, and such a blessing to hear."

"I'd really like to honor and glorify God in our relationship, Afton. I'd love for Him to look down from Heaven and see us together and smile because I'm blessing you, encouraging you in your faith, and pointing you to Him. And you're doing the same with me. Wouldn't that be beautiful?"

"So beautiful." Afton's eyes were moist with emotion. "I'd love that, Dakota."

"And I want you to know that I'm not the kind of person who would date you just for fun or to have a girlfriend. I've held off on dating anyone because I only want to date someone that I'd seriously be interested in marrying someday."

"I feel the same way, Dakota. Let's turn left here at the crosswalk."

"And I know most teens in our shoes would probably already be kissing each other, but I think we should wait. I mean, I'd *love* to kiss you, but I think we should take things slow . . . make sure we're really a good match for each other."

"I agree, Dakota. I'd love to kiss you too. But that can wait. I'm just happy to hold your hand. Can we keep doing that?"

"For sure. And I'd even say hugs are okay if you're okay with that."

Afton stopped, turned to Dakota, and they embraced in a long hug.

"This is the best hug I've ever had, Mr. Knox."

"Likewise, Miss Hansley. . . . I'd like to pray for us. Would you mind?"

"Please."

They put their foreheads against each other's, looked into one another's eyes, and closed them.

"Heavenly Father, we love You. I thank You for this special girl and our friendship. And You see that we're starting a new chapter together as boyfriend and girlfriend. God, we want to honor You. We want to bless You with all that we say and do. Will You be the center of our relationship? We want everything to revolve around *You*. We are living for You. We belong to You. Deliver us from evil. Sanctify us. Keep us for Yourself. Guide us in Your will and whatever *You'd* like to do with our lives. And it's in Jesus's name, we pray. Amen."

"Amen."

They opened their eyes.

"I love you, Afton."

"I love you."

"You have the prettiest green eyes on the planet. Do you know that?"

"You're sweet. Thank you. Your blue eyes have taken my breath away more than once."

"Ha! We're in love." Dakota said.

"We are."

Afton spun out of the hug with Dakota's hand in hers, and the two briefly danced to the thumping bass and drumbeat coming from a nearby nightclub. They continued walking.

A short while later, Afton said, "We're going to pass right by my uncle's hotel. Maybe we should poke our heads in real quick and say 'hey.'"

"Let's!"

# Chapter 13

Back at the Marriott, Eeman sat by the fourth-floor window, bored and perturbed. He looked at Ahmed asleep on the couch. *This is ridiculous. I'm sick of looking out the window. Dakota must have checked out, or he rarely leaves his room.*

But a few minutes later, Eeman spotted Dakota and Afton holding hands and walking toward the hotel.

"Ahmed, wake up! Here they come."

Ahmed opened his eyes.

Eeman grabbed his Smith & Wesson .45 caliber handgun off the table and pulled open the window. He pointed the black barrel with its noise-muzzling silencer at Dakota. As he aligned the sights on Dakota's chest, he muttered, "You've breathed your last, you little punk."

Eeman pulled the trigger.

There was no discharge.

"Arghhh! I forgot to rack a round in the chamber."

"Seriously?" Ahmed said as he scrambled to grab his own gun.

Eeman quickly yanked the slide back on his gun, but it was too late. Dakota and Afton walked through the front door.

"Dang it!"

"Quick. Let's go," Ahmed said. "Maybe we can catch them downstairs walking through the lobby."

The two men ran out the door, darted down the hallway, and waited for the elevator.

• • •

"Here's the hotel," Afton said. "This will be quick."

The two teens walked into the lobby.

"This is a nice hotel," Dakota said.

"Isn't it?"

Afton didn't see her uncle at the reception desk. She inquired about him with a young lady behind the counter.

"He's back here in his office. I'll tell him you're here."

A minute later, Chad looked around the corner. He was talking on his phone but waved Afton and Dakota into his office and motioned for them to have a seat.

• • •

The elevator opened on the ground floor. Ahmed and Eeman looked right and left, hoping to find Dakota and Afton waiting to get on. No sight of them.

They scoured the lobby.

"They must have already got on the lift," Eeman said. "Maybe we can nab them walking in a hall. Let's go. We'll stop at every floor and quickly look."

They ran to the elevator.

• • •

Afton's uncle Chad hung up his phone and smiled at his niece. "What brings you two by?"

"We went out for dinner at The Shard and were walking home, right by here, so I thought we'd just pop in and say hi."

"Well, that was nice of you guys. It's been a busy night. Sorry I was on the phone."

"No worries, Uncle Chad."

"Thanks again for picking us up from the airport," Dakota said.

"You're welcome. Happy to help."

They chatted with him for a couple of minutes and said goodnight.

When they arrived back at Bryanston Square, Dakota said, "I'll walk you up to your place."

"Thank you. . . . Dakota, this truly has been the best day ever," Afton said as they stood at her front door. "I enjoyed spending every minute of it with you. Breakfast, the Sherlock Holmes Museum, riding bikes, everything. I can't imagine a better day with a better person."

"It really was the best day ever with the best tour guide ever. Thank you."

They curled their arms around each other. As they held each other, Afton said, "Can I pray for us?"

"Of course."

"Dear Lord, this has been the best day today. Thank You. We know that every good and perfect gift comes from You, so we thank You for every blessing we enjoyed today. The good food, the sunshine, safe travels, our new relationship as girlfriend and boyfriend. What a blessing. We love You. We praise You! Thank You for loving us. We pray for Your blessing on our lives and our sleep tonight. And it's in the name of our glorious Savior and Shepherd, King Jesus, we pray. Amen."

"Amen. I love your prayers, Afton—you're a dream come true. I love you. Sleep well."

"Sleep well, Mr. Knox. I'll talk to you in the morning. And send me those pictures of us at The Shard when you're able. I want to see your cute face every time I pick up my phone."

"Will do. Talk soon."

# Chapter 14
## Thursday morning, June 23, London.

The following morning, Afton rolled over in her bed and reached for her phone. She was delighted to see a message from Dakota.

> **Dakota:** Good morning, my love. Was yesterday a dream? Pinch me. You're my girlfriend, and I'm head over heels in love with you Afton Hansley! Here are the pictures of us at The Shard. I wish we would have taken more throughout the day. I was having too much fun to think about photos.

> **Afton:** Good morning. I just woke up, and you were the first thing on my mind. I love you!! I'm so happy to be your girlfriend. Thanks for the pics. I'm putting one on my home screen right now.

> **Dakota:** Same. Do you have any plans today?

> **Afton:** No. I'm yours. Take me away, Mr. Knox. Let's do something fun.

> **Dakota:** You're amazing.

**Afton:** I think our families are doing something today.

**Dakota:** Actually, I just talked to my mom. She and Hank don't feel good.

**Afton:** Oh, I'm sorry. I'll pray for them.

**Dakota:** So, they need to stay home again.

**Afton:** How do you feel?

**Dakota:** Never better. I feel like I could dance.

**Afton:** Come dance with me.

**Dakota:** I want to. What should we do today? What would bless you?

**Afton:** I think you'd love the British Museum. I haven't been in a few years. That seems fun to me.

**Dakota:** I'd love that!

**Afton:** You're easy. It's about a mile-and-a-half walk. We can stop somewhere on the way and get coffee and muffins if you'd like.

**Dakota:** Perfect.

**Afton:** Why don't we meet outside at 9:30? The museum

opens at 10:00.

**Dakota:** 9:30 is good.

**Afton:** Probably should wear a light jacket. If you haven't looked outside yet, it's cold and drizzly out. Looks like it could rain. I'll bring an umbrella.

**Dakota:** I'll wear a jacket. See you soon.

# Chapter 15
## Thursday morning, June 23, Marriott Hotel.

As Dakota and Afton prepared for their outing to the British Museum, Eeman monitored the hotel's entrance from the **Marriott's** fourth-floor window. Ahmed sat in his bed sipping coffee and watching *Good Morning Britain*.

"Your hair, Eeman. Wow. It's out of control."

"Are we participating in a fashion show today? No."

"Hey, surely, you have a live round in the chamber this morning."

"Of course."

"You didn't last night! So, we'll keep an eye on the entrance for a while, and then we need to go pick up the Audi from impound."

"Why don't you go get it right now?" Eeman asked. "And I'll stay here."

"We have to wait 24 hours before we can pick it up."

*–P O O M!*

"Whoa!"

"What the heck, Eeman! You fired your gun?"

"Dang it! I was just spinning it on my finger a little bit. I must have pulled the trigger."

"Spinning it on your finger? Really? Is this why the U.S. was able to topple Baghdad so easily in two thousand three?"

"Our training sucked."

"I can tell. Where'd the bullet go?"

"I don't know."

Ahmed noticed white dust falling from the ceiling.

"You shot a hole through the ceiling! Idiot!"

"Oops."

"Grab your stuff, and let's go. You might have killed some-body above us, and now the police are going to come and investigate."

"Sorry, Ahmed."

"Hurry up!"

The two men grabbed their belongings and bolted out the door.

"Where are we going, Ahmed?"

"Somewhere the cops aren't. I don't know yet."

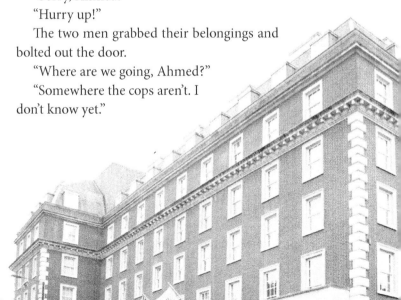

# Chapter 16
## Thursday morning, June 23, 9:30 a.m.
## Bryanston Square, London.

Dakota and Afton met outside on the wet sidewalk and hugged.

"Good morning. I like this black jacket, Dakota."

"Thanks. I got it at the surf shop where I used to work. I'm glad I packed it. I can't believe the drizzly weather in June."

"That's London. We usually get two-to-three inches of rain in June. I brought an umbrella, just in case. Shall we head out?"

"Lead the way, Miss Hansley."

"Hand, please."

A few minutes later, they stopped in a café and picked up coffees and warm apple-cinnamon muffins.

"Delicious!" Dakota said as they continued walking. "Did you tell your mom about our day yesterday?"

"I did. She's happy for us."

"So is my mom."

"Oh, good."

"I don't know why but going to a museum on a drizzly day with a warm drink and the girl of my dreams by my side just seems like the best day ever, part two."

"Same, Dakota. And aren't you excited to see some of the archaeological artifacts that connect to Biblical events?"

"I am."

As they approached the **British Museum's** south entrance, Dakota looked up at the massive Greek-temple-inspired columns along the front of the buildings. "Whoa. This museum is gigantic."

"Enormous. You're going to love it."

They made their way up the stairs and walked inside. The museum was buzzing with people. Everywhere they meandered were sculptures and busts of Egyptian pharaohs, mummies, and hundreds of artifacts from ancient Assyria, Greece, and Rome.

Dakota and Afton noticed a couple of men standing near a video camera on a tripod. In front of the camera was an older man wearing glasses and a light gray sports coat.

One of the cameramen stepped in between him and the camera with a clapperboard and said, "Gilgamesh Epic flood tablet. Take one."

Dakota whispered, "Let's back up a bit so we don't distract him."

The man in the sports coat said, "The Bible tells us that God judged the ancient world for their widespread wickedness with a cataclysmic flood that devastated the planet. If this event happened as Moses said and as Jesus and Peter affirmed, surely there should be some evidence for it. And there is. Allow me to share with you a quick overview of two different lines of evidence for the flood.

"First, everywhere archaeologists and geologists dig on all seven continents, they find billions of dead creatures buried and fossilized inside sedimentary rock made up of sand, mud, and lime that was deposited rapidly by water.

"Billions of dead creatures encased inside rock that was laid down by water? That's odd. Animals that die natural deaths rapidly decompose and disappear. That's what happens to animals when they die. Their bodies fall to the ground, and within months their bones are dragged off by scavengers, or, if left alone, they begin to decay under the wear and tear of the elements. But something different happened with the billions of creatures we find in the fossil record. Their bones are preserved, many of them wholly intact with very little evidence of decay. This has led many paleontologists, geologists, and archaeologists to conclude that these creatures were killed during a flood. Their bodies were caught in the mudflow, rapidly buried in the sediment while it was still wet and soft, and then preserved.

"The fossils of billions of dead creatures encased in sedimentary rock all over the world are a powerful reminder of the flood described in the Book of Genesis.

"In addition to the widespread fossil evidence, archaeologists have unearthed several ancient non-Biblical writings *describing* a catastrophic flood.

"Of course, after the flood, as Noah's descendants spread out to different parts of the world, they took their memories of the flood with them and passed those memories down to their kids, who passed them down to their kids, and on and on it went. And so it comes as no surprise that the Sumerians, Assyrians, Babylonians, Greeks, Hindus, Chinese, Mexicans,

Algonquins, and Hawaiians all have ancient accounts of a devastating flood.

"There are more than two hundred ancient accounts of a catastrophic flood *outside* the Bible—95% of them indicating that the flood was global in its scope.

"Although there are some differences among the accounts, the parallels are striking. Consider this list of similarities between the flood account in the Book of Genesis and this ancient tablet here at the British Museum that relates part of the **Epic of Gilgamesh**. It was unearthed in the ancient ruins of a library at Nineveh in northern Iraq. It dates to the seventh century BC.

"In both accounts:

> –the flood was divinely planned
> –the flood was related to the defection of the human race from God or the gods
> –advance notice of the flood was given to one individual
> –there was instruction to build a boat
> –the boat was covered inside and out with a waterproofing pitch (a tar-like substance)
> –a storm brought on the flood
> –the boat builder's family and animals aboard the boat survived
> –everyone not on the boat was destroyed

–the boat came to rest atop a mountain

–birds were sent out after the flood to determine if the world was habitable

–and sacrifices were offered after the flood

"Well! With so many points in common between the Gilgamesh Epic and the Biblical account, it is not difficult to conclude (as many scholars have) that both accounts recall a common event: the devastating **flood** recorded in the Book of Genesis."

When the man finished speaking, Dakota squeezed Afton's hand. "That was amazing. He sounds like a Christian. We should meet him."

"Let's!"

They approached the man. "Hi, my name is Dakota Knox. This is my girlfriend, Afton."

"I'm Alistair Fernsby. Nice to meet you both."

"I really enjoyed what you had to say about the Epic of Gilgamesh and evidence for the flood," Dakota said.

"Thank you."

"You sound like a Christian."

"I am. We're making a documentary on archaeological evidence that corroborates the Bible."

"That's amazing!" Dakota said.

"I'm starting college in a couple of months, and I'll be studying to be an archaeologist," Afton said. "Are you an archaeologist or—?"

"Yes, I'm an archaeologist and a retired professor."

"Oh, wow, it's so nice to meet you," Afton said. "We're

Christians, too, and we love archaeology. We were just in Israel exploring Caesarea and Masada and—"

"I've worked on excavations in Israel. It's a pleasure to meet two young people interested in the Bible and archaeology." The man looked at his watch. "I don't want to cut our talk short, but we only have so long to film inside the museum, and we still have two more artifacts to do. Would you like to follow us and listen in?"

"Absolutely!" Afton said.

The two teens walked with the archaeologist to the next artifact. A man readied the camera and lighting while Alistair glanced at some notes. When he was ready, the man with the clapperboard stood in front of the camera and said, "Nabonidus—Babylonian Chronicle Tablet. Filming in three, two, one."

Alistair Fernsby smiled and said, "Daniel 5:1 tells us that Belshazzar the king of Babylon made a great feast for a thousand of his lords and drank wine in the presence of the thousand.

"While this massive party was going on, Belshazzar saw a human hand write a mysterious message on the wall that no one was able to interpret. Daniel was called in to help interpret the message, and the interpretation indicated that Belshazzar's kingdom was done. God had had enough of the wicked king. And the Bible tells us that Belshazzar was killed that night, and the city of Babylon passed into the hands of the Medes and Persians.

"An ancient Greek historian named Herodotus tells us that the Persians gained entry into Babylon by diverting the Euphrates River (that flowed into the city) and coming in through its riverbed.

"Well, this passage of Scripture, Daniel 5, was long the target of critics' cannons. They considered Daniel's references to Belshazzar 'pure invention' and a 'historical blunder.' Why? The name Belshazzar could not be found anywhere outside the Bible, and ancient historians Berossus and Alexander Polyhistor said the last king of the Babylonian empire was a man named *not* Belshazzar but *Nabonidus*. And so critics of the Bible insisted for years that the author of the Book of Daniel just made up the name Belshazzar.

"And a lot of people believed them until this inscription was found. This **Babylonian tablet** here at the British Museum tells us that when king Nabonidus left Babylon for a multi-year stay in the Arabian oasis town of Tema (about four hundred and fifty miles away from Babylon), he entrusted the rule of Babylon into the hands of *Belshazzar*, his eldest son.

"What do you know! Daniel *was* right. Sometimes it just takes historians and archaeologists thousands of years to catch up with the Bible."

Dakota wanted to clap. He turned to Afton and said, "Mr. Fernsby knows his stuff. I've read about that discovery, but the facts just roll off his lips like he owns the information."

"Very impressive."

"He would be a good person to know, Afton. Maybe he could connect you with excavation opportunities . . . give you helpful advice."

"For sure. Let's get his card when he's done. Have I told you that I love you lately?" Afton asked.

"It's been a few minutes."

"Well, I love you."

"I love you too."

"All right, lovebirds," Mr. Fernsby said, "follow me—one more artifact down this way."

When the camera was in place, and the red light was flashing, Alistair said, "This six-sided clay prism unearthed at Nineveh is known as the **Taylor Prism**. It mentions the Assyrian King Sennacherib's invasion of Judah during the reign of King Hezekiah and corroborates several details in 2 Kings 18–19 and Isaiah 36–37. This short paragraph on the Taylor Prism confirms at least six details in the Biblical account:

–Hezekiah was a real person
–Jews lived in Jerusalem at the time of Sennacherib's rule (705–681 BC)
–Judah was a legitimate kingdom with many "strong, walled cities" and "small cities"
–Hezekiah lived in "his royal city," Jerusalem, confirming he was also a king
–Hezekiah "did not submit" to Sennacherib's initial demands

    –Sennacherib invaded the land of Judah on a military
    campaign to stop the revolt

Alistair Fernsby went on for a couple of minutes, explaining the artifact's significance. When he finished, the cameraman said, "That's a wrap. Nailed it, Dr. Fernsby. Great job!"

Afton and Dakota thanked the archaeologist and his team for letting them tag along and listen in. He gave Afton his business card and invited her to contact him if he could ever be of assistance. After looking at some more artifacts, the two teens decided to head out for lunch and save the rest of the museum for another day.

"There's a little café a few blocks south of here with sandwiches, soup, salads, and smoothies. Does that sound good?"

"It does," Dakota said.

"We can get the food to go and bring it down to Victoria Embankment Gardens. It's a pretty park by the river."

"I love that idea."

"I love you."

They walked outside and down the steps of the museum.

"Look at that. The sun's out!" Afton stretched up her arms to the sky and spun around to playfully dance with Dakota. "Is this what southern California feels like in the summer?"

"Add 20 degrees."

They turned right at the museum's main gate, grabbed each other's hands, and strolled south along the busy sidewalk.

"How cool was that—meeting Dr. Fernsby?"

"So cool!" Dakota said.

"I feel even more inspired to pursue the field of archaeology. Think of the millions of Christians and non-Christians who don't know about these discoveries! And I'm sure there are thousands of additional discoveries waiting to be found."

"For sure."

Dakota and Afton stopped at the café. They walked out ten minutes later with sandwiches and smoothies and continued south toward Victoria Embankment Gardens.

# Chapter 17

While the café was preparing Dakota and Afton's order, Eeman and Ahmed came up from the London Underground at the Covent Garden Station, a ten-minute walk south of the British Museum.

"It will be good to get the car back, Ahmed."

"Yeah, my app says the impound place is a few more blocks this way and then a couple of blocks to the east."

As they walked north on Drury Lane, Ahmed explained what the new plan was for tracking down Dakota.

"Staying at the hotel is not going to be an option after your brainless discharge of the gun. After we retrieve Radomir's Audi, we're going to go—"

"Ahmed, did you—"

"Don't interrupt me. I'm thinking this through. We're going to go back to Grosvenor Square and monitor the hotel entrance from the car. Or maybe we—"

"Ahmed, I think you should know that—"

"Hold on. I'm working out our options! Maybe we rent bikes and ride around the hotel . . . Hmm. What were you going to say, Eeman?"

"I was going to say that a couple that passed us a minute or two ago looked like Dakota and the girl!"

Eeman stopped walking. "Serious?"

"Yeah. The guy was wearing jeans, a black jacket, and a brown and yellow baseball cap—the same one he had on yesterday at Buckingham Palace."

"Let's go! What was the girl wearing?"

"Black jeans and a light brown coat, black sunglasses. They were carrying small bags, maybe food."

The men jogged south along Drury Lane, weaving in and out of people.

• • •

"Oh, boy. Afton, don't look now, but we're being followed."

"Followed?"

"Yep, and I'm pretty sure it's the same two guys we encountered at Buckingham Palace. I don't think they work for the King." Dakota could feel his heart beating faster. "Let's speed up and cross the street."

"Embankment Gardens is pretty popular," Afton said. "Maybe they're headed there too."

"I don't think that's what's happening."

Dakota and Afton quickly crossed the street and went around the corner and out of view of the two men.

"Let's jog," Dakota said. After about fifty yards, he looked over his shoulder, and the two men came running around the corner.

"Drop the food, Afton. We have to run fast. They're coming. Stay with me!"

"Okay!"

Dakota and Afton turned a corner, darted between cars, and zigzagged between people coming in the opposite direction. The two men did the same.

Afton held her phone up. "Hey, Siri, call 9-1-1!"

Afton and Dakota made a right and sprinted down an alley. The passage was about a hundred yards long, lined with trash cans, and free of pedestrians. Halfway toward a clearing, they heard several loud gunshots behind them.

"Dakota! They're shooting at us."

"I heard. Stay low."

"This must be related to the missing artifacts in Israel!" Afton said.

"I'm thinking the same thing! I'm sorry."

Two more gunshots went off. Dakota heard residents screaming and shutting their windows.

They reached the end of the alley, made a hard right turn, and ran toward Victoria Embankment Gardens. They sprinted into the park at the east end and raced past a statue of a man holding a Bible.

"That's the Robert Raikes statue," Afton shouted. "He was the pioneer of Sunday schools for children back in the seventeen hundreds."

Dakota yelled, "Only the world's best tour guide would tell someone that when she's being shot at and chased by murderers!"

The quaint city park with lawns and gardens was teeming with people.

Dakota and Afton dodged people left and right.

"Sorry, everybody!" Dakota said.

Afton spoke into her phone as she ran. "Yes . . . we're being chased through Victoria Embankment Gardens by two men with guns. . . . No, *we* don't have guns, they do!"

Several people who heard her scattered, looking for places to hide.

Dakota and Afton angled across the grass, jumped over flowerbeds, and made a beeline to an exit gate at the southwest end of the park.

"Pardon us, please!"

"Coming through on your right."

"Excuse us. . . . So sorry."

The two men stayed on their trail like bloodhounds about a stone's throw behind them.

Dakota and Afton made a right at the street and crossed three busy lanes of traffic.

People barked, "Watch where you're going! Use the crosswalk!"

"Sorry! Follow me, Afton."

They went up a few steps and down a ramp to a covered dock on the River Thames called "Embankment Pier." It was crowded with people and had a large sightseeing boat and a couple of smaller boats lined up against it.

"I trust you have a plan, Dakota—because this pier is a dead end."

"I always have a plan, Miss Hansley. Whether it's a good one is another question. I'm thinking we jump in the water and swim or hide under the dock until the police show up."

The two teens cut through the line of people and scooted past the ticket collector.

"Hey! You can't do that. You both need tickets."

"Not today!" Dakota said.

A couple of seconds before they would have jumped into the water, Dakota spotted two speedboats full of people about to embark on a "Speedboat River Tour of London." The one in front was slowly pulling away from the dock.

"Change of plans, Afton! Follow me." Dakota jumped into the boat and held out his hand to help Afton with her landing.

The boat driver at the rear of the boat said, "Out! This boat only seats twelve people."

"My apologies," Dakota said, "but if you don't pull out of here right now, this boat is going to be shot to smithereens, and we could all die!"

People in the boat panicked and began leaping into the water and back onto the dock.

Dakota tried to clarify. "*I* don't have a gun." He looked back at the dock and pointed. "*That* guy does!"

One of the two men was making his way through the line of people with his gun out. "Out of my way!"

People screamed and looked for ways to escape.

The man looked directly at Dakota, crouching down in the boat about fifteen feet away from the dock. He fired two shots.

Dakota yelled at the driver, "Go, go!" He and Afton hid behind the boat's starboard side.

The boat driver ducked and shoved the throttle lever forward. Dakota heard and felt the roar of the 740-horsepower engine as the bow lifted and they took off.

Dakota looked back at the dock. Everyone was fleeing, except the man with the gun. "Afton, the gunman is getting in the other speedboat."

"Oh, no," she said. "God, please keep us safe!"

"Amen. I don't know where the second guy went."

Dakota tenderly held Afton's face in his hands and looked into her eyes. Their faces were dripping with the salty spray coming over the boat's sides. "I don't know what's going to happen to us, Miss Hansley. But no matter what happens, I want you to know that I *love* you. I'm *crazy* about you—"

"I'm crazy about you too, Dakota."

"If we die, we'll walk through the gates of splendor together. If I die alone, I'll be waiting for you in Heaven, and we'll continue the adventure there. Okay?"

"Okay."

"Sir!" Dakota yelled, "Drive this thing like you stole it! That guy chasing us is going to try to kill us."

The driver glanced over his shoulder. The other boat was about seventy-five yards behind them. He looked

back at Dakota and said, "I'm sorry. I have a wife and kids!" He stood and jumped off the boat into the river.

Dakota and Afton looked at each other in disbelief—the boat was racing west up the Thames, *driverless*. Dakota crawled over to the exposed platform at the stern. He reached up and tried to steer the boat without standing and exposing himself to possible gunfire.

"Dakota, angle to the right," Afton yelled. "We're headed toward the bridge!"

Dakota realized he'd have to stand to steer the boat and see over the bow. They'd crash if he didn't. He stood and turned the steering wheel to the right, narrowly missing a massive concrete bridge support. *Phew!* **Big Ben** and the **Parliament building** flew by on the right. Dakota turned and looked. The other boat was still about seventy-five yards behind them. *It's going to be hard to lose someone driving a boat with the same size engine. I think when I see another sandy beach, I'll—*

His thoughts were interrupted by the sound of two more gunshots.

"Afton! When there's a sandy beach, I'm going to run the boat ashore. We'll jump out, use the boat for a bit of cover if we need to, and take off into the city. Be ready to jump out, okay?"

She nodded.

About a minute later, Dakota said, "I think I see a beach about a hundred yards ahead. Stay down until I say."

Dakota looked over his shoulder. The other boat was about fifty yards behind theirs. He turned the steering wheel and angled the boat towards the shore on the northern side of the river. Knowing the vessel would come to a sudden stop, Dakota pulled the throttle back, but they were still coming in fast. When the boat hit the sand, it came to a jolting halt.

"Sorry about that, Afton. You, okay?"

"Yep."

"Let's go!"

Dakota and Afton jumped out of the boat and ran up the wet sand toward a break in the wall. Behind the break was a narrow walkway with cement steps leading up to the street. Dakota looked back. The gunman landed the second boat on the sand, jumped out, and fired off a couple of rounds toward the two teens.

Dakota and Afton cut across a busy street, ran through the first floor of a parking structure, and sprinted down a residential street.

The man was still on their trail. They shed their wet coats and ran as fast as they could.

"Let's go this way to the left," Dakota said.

"No, Dakota! That's a dead end!"

It was too late. The two teens were separated. Afton continued running straight, and Dakota had already committed to going left. Reversing course would mean a face-to-face encounter with the gunman.

The man pursued Dakota down the alley.

Dakota realized he had made a terrible decision. "Oh, no. I'm sorry, Afton."

No answer.

He turned around. She wasn't there.

But there *was* one person behind him . . . the gunman.

He looked like he was in his early thirties and perhaps from somewhere in the Middle East. He walked toward Dakota, pointing his gun at him. Drips of river water or sweat ran down his unshaven face to the collar of his black tee shirt. Now that Dakota saw him up close, he recognized him as one of the men from Buckingham Palace and the driver of the car that had tried to run them off the road two days earlier.

Dakota looked around for something to fight with or hide behind. There was nothing but a couple of street light posts, small shrubs, and a few plastic trash cans.

*Oh boy. God, You're going to have to help me. I've hit a dead end.*

"Ah, the little troublemaker from California," the gunman said. "Where are you going to run now? There's nowhere to go."

Dakota slowly backed up, thinking of what to do. He yelled out to any residents who might be in their townhomes on his right or left. "Is anyone home? Call the police! There's a madman out here with a gun."

No one responded. The man continued to walk closer,

holding his gun with both hands.

Cornered with a diminishing set of options, Dakota made a split-second decision to duck and run right at him.

The man fired a shot. It missed.

Dakota tackled the man to the pavement and violently shook the gun out of his hand. He held down the man's right arm, and with a clenched right fist, bashed the man's left cheek and nose. After five or six blows, Dakota saw the man's gun lying about six feet away on the ground. He rolled off the man and grabbed the gun. He stood, planning to run back toward where he and Afton had been separated. But he was confronted by the return of the bloodied man's sidekick, a tall, muscular man with black curly hair.

Dakota pointed the barrel of his friend's gun at him. "What do you want from me?"

"I want my pizza!" the man said and laughed.

"What! Get on the ground, or I'll shoot," Dakota yelled.

The man on the ground with blood coming out of his nose stood and said, "Eeman, take him down. That's *my* gun, and it's out of bullets."

Dakota looked at the gun. The slide was open, indicating that it *was* out of ammo.

"My gun's out of ammo too," the muscular man said.

Dakota flipped the empty gun around and held it by the barrel, intending to use it as a hammer-like weapon.

The man in front of him laughed, reached behind his back side, pulled out a Taser gun, and pulled the trigger. Two metal darts hit Dakota in the chest and sent a painful blast of electricity through his body. The pistol fell to the ground. Dakota dropped to the pavement. Everything went black.

Ahmed got up and wiped some blood off his face. "Nice one, Eeman. Glad you were able to track me here."

"Oh wow, that kid got you good, Ahmed. Your face!"

Ahmed kicked Dakota in the ribs. "I'll be fine."

"Okay. Watch him. I'll be right back."

"What's going on down there?" a woman yelled. "Is everyone okay?"

"No reason for alarm," Ahmed hollered back. "Everyone's okay—we're with MI-5. This guy tried to plant a bomb at the parliament building, but we got him. All is well. Go about your business."

"Well, thank you! Our family appreciates the work you guys do."

"You're welcome."

A silver Lexus sedan sped around the corner and stopped next to Dakota. The trunk popped open, and Eeman opened the driver's side door.

Ahmed rubbed his hand along the hood. "Where'd you get this?"

"Some lady near Embankment Pier. I tapped my gun on her window and told her to get out."

Eeman bent down and started to lift Dakota's unconscious body. "Get his legs and help me throw him in the trunk."

"Hold on. I need to get his phone out, or they'll track his location." Ahmed pulled Dakota's phone from his jeans and looked at it. There were several messages on the lock screen:

**Afton:** Where are you? I'm around the corner.

**Afton:** Are you there?

**Afton:** Dakota? I love you.

**Afton:** Are you okay? I'll come and find you.

Ahmed laughed. "Nope." He held the phone up to Dakota's face. It recognized his face and unlocked. Ahmed replied to Afton's messages:

**Dakota:** I'm okay, but I'm super disappointed that you abandoned me. I never want to see you again. We're done.

Ahmed was delighted with the sinister idea. He tapped send, turned the phone off, and dropped it through a metal grate into the sewer.

The two men lifted Dakota's body, set it in the trunk, and closed it. They hopped into the front seats, backed out of the alley, and sped off.

# Chapter 18

Afton peeked her head around the corner of a building a minute after she and Dakota were separated. *I have no idea where the gunman went. I hope Dakota's okay. What should I do?* She sent him a text.

> **Afton:** Dakota, where are you? I'm around the corner.

No response. A moment later, she heard Dakota yell, "Is anyone home? Call the police. There's a madman out here with a gun."

Seconds later, she heard a single gunshot. *Oh, no. God— please protect Dakota!*

> **Afton:** Are you there?

> **Afton:** Dakota? I love you.

> **Afton:** Are you okay? I'll come and find you.

Afton carefully walked toward the danger. *If he's been shot, I need to help him.*

She received a message from Dakota:

> **Dakota:** I'm okay, but I'm super disappointed that you abandoned me. I never want to see you again. We're done.

Dakota's words took the breath out of her lungs. She reread it three times. *How could he think that? We're done? No. Lord, what's happened? How could he believe I abandoned him?*

She messaged him back.

> **Afton:** It was an accident. I love you, Dakota. We were running so fast, and I didn't want us to get stuck in a cul-de-sac with nowhere to go. I thought you heard me say that was a dead end, and I assumed you followed me. But when I looked back, you weren't there.

There was no response. She walked faster toward the cul-de-sac. *He's got to be over there still. Maybe he disarmed the gunman and killed him? Perhaps that's what the gunshot was. And if so, he'll wait for the police to show up so he can explain what happened.*

She rounded the corner, hoping to see him standing there. He wasn't.

She walked down the street where Dakota had been. No gunman, no Dakota.

Afton yelled out, "Dakota!"

No answer.

She looked behind bushes.

"Dakota, it's me! It's safe to come out." *I'm so confused.* She reread Dakota's text:

> **Dakota:** I'm okay, but I'm super disappointed that you abandoned me. I never want to see you again. We're done.

She sat on the curb and sobbed. *I can't believe this. How did this happen? He's done with me? He just told me on the boat, 'No matter what happens, I want you to know that I love you. I'm crazy about you!' I don't understand what's going on, Lord. I'm crushed. And now he's gone? I don't know what to do.*

A police car pulled up at the curb next to her. A female officer got out and introduced herself. Her name was Madeline. With tears in her eyes, Afton explained all that had happened. Madeline hugged her. "You're going to be okay. I bet after Dakota recovers from the trauma of being shot at, he'll think more clearly about what happened, and you two will be good as new."

"Thank you."

"These other officers are going to investigate the crime scene. May I give you a ride home?"

Afton nodded yes. "Thank you."

"You're welcome, honey. Hop in my car."

On the drive through the bustling streets of London, Afton kept an eye out for Dakota, hoping to spot him walking home.

No sight of him.

She kept glancing at her phone, hoping to see a text from him.

Nothing.

She called him. When his voicemail greeting came on, she ended the call and sent him a text:

> **Afton:** Hi Dakota. I'm really sorry. Where are you? Are you walking home? A nice police officer is driving me home. Can we talk once you're home? Can we pick you up somewhere?

No response. Afton couldn't keep from crying.

*Oh, God. I don't know what's going on. Will You help Dakota think clearly about what happened? Will You help him forgive me? I love that guy! Bless him. Bless us. Help him to make it back safely. Help the police officers find those men. I thought they were in Israel, but I guess they followed us here. We need You. Protect our families and dads in Israel. This is crazy! First, the assassination attempt in Israel, and now guys are shooting at us in London. We came here to get away from the madness. We need Your help in Jesus's name.*

When they arrived at Bryanston Square, Madeline walked Afton to her door.

"Here's my card, Afton, with my number. Call me if I can answer any questions for you, okay? And we'll be reaching out to you soon too."

"Okay, thank you."

Madeline gave Afton a hug.

Afton opened the door. "Hello. Is anyone home? Mom? Evelyn? Ethan?"

No answer. She walked to her bedroom, collapsed on her white down comforter, and cried.

Ten minutes later, she checked her phone—still no response from Dakota.

*That's so rude! Now, I'm mad. He should at least respond and assure me that he's still safe. He said he was okay, but still! I'll text his mom and see if he's come home yet.*

**Afton:** Hi Mrs. Knox. Afton here. I hope you're feeling better. Has Dakota come home yet?

112

**Abigail:** Hi Afton. No. I thought he was with you. How was the British Museum? Did you guys have fun?

**Afton:** It was fine, but some crazy things happened afterward. Can I call you?

**Abigail:** Please do.

Afton explained to Mrs. Knox what had happened. She was horrified.

"Oh, dear. Thank you for telling me, Afton. I'm so glad you're okay. I'm going to call Madeline and get an update and more details. And we'll pray that Dakota comes walking through our front door soon!"

"That's what I'm praying too."

"And Afton, that text about Dakota being 'done' with you doesn't sound like him. He told me earlier today how much he *loves* you. So, something isn't right. Maybe he wrote it under duress. Maybe someone pressured him to type that. It just doesn't sound like anything he'd say."

"I know," Afton said, all choked up.

"I love you, sweet girl. God's going to bring us through this. Try to get hold of your mom again, and we'll talk soon. Come over if you'd like."

"Thank you, Mrs. Knox. I love you too."

# Chapter 19

Dakota opened his eyes. It was dark. His neck was kinked, and the right side of his face was on fabric that felt rough against his skin. *Where am I?*

The air was stuffy and warm.

He felt nauseous. His skin was sweaty.

*My chest hurts. My knuckles hurt. I'm so thirsty. Why can't I see? Hold on.*

He felt around with his hands. Whatever he was in was lined with a felt-like material. Above him was metal. He could hear a noise that sounded like a car's engine.

*I'm in the trunk of a car! Oh, no. Those guys threw me in a trunk? Where are they taking me? I've got to get out of here. They're going to kill me.*

*I should pray. God, You see what's going on. Your Word says, 'there is no creature hidden from Your sight, and that 'all things are open and laid bare to the eyes of Him to whom we must answer.' So, I'm glad You see me, and You see what these evil men are planning to do, and one day, they will answer for it. But for now, I ask for deliverance, strength, courage, wisdom. You delivered Daniel out of the lion's den. I pray You'll deliver me, and I also pray for Afton—thank You for her. I don't know what happened to her. I hope she's okay. Bless her! Guide her home safely. Amen.*

He laid there on his side wondering, *why didn't they kill me? They said they were out of ammo. What should I do?*

He thought about his options.

*I'll disconnect the brake light and blinker bulbs! Maybe a highway patrolman will pull him over. My dad showed me how to change out the bulbs. It wasn't hard.*

He felt around for the panel on the driver's side and pulled it off. That allowed a little natural light into the trunk. *Now I can see better.*

Dakota disconnected two small bulbs, adjusted his body, and did the same thing on the passenger side.

*What else can I do?*

*Where's my phone?* He reached into his pocket. *I must have lost it. Bummer! It had all my Israel photos on it with Afton.*

He looked around, hoping to find anything that might help him. There was a folder with some papers in it and a folded blanket. *Those won't be helpful. Hold on, what's this? A plastic handle on the floor of the trunk.* Dakota lifted it. Underneath was a storage compartment. There was a first-aid kit, a quart of oil, a crescent wrench, a rag, a candle, a box of matches, four plastic bottles of water, and three granola bars.

*Hallelujah!*

Dakota cranked the plastic lid off a bottle of water and chugged the entire thing. *I don't think water has ever tasted so good!*

He tore open a granola bar and devoured it in two or three bites. *Thank you, God. What should I do when these wicked men open the trunk? Fight? I could use this wrench. Or should I go along peacefully, then fight? Maybe I'll pretend to be dead, then surprise them when they try to pull me out.*

He had a plethora of ideas.

About thirty minutes after he woke up, Dakota felt the car slow down, make a left turn, and stop. The car moved forward again up a curvy road with tiny bumps. When the hill leveled off, the vehicle came to a stop.

Dakota decided he would get out of the car peacefully and pretend to go along with whatever the captor or captors wanted before launching a surprise attack. He put the last granola bar in his pocket and the wrench within reach.

When the car stopped, Dakota heard two men talking in the front seat.

"Why don't we walk him down to the pond and shoot him there? And then I can bury him and Avner in the same hole."

"That'll work. I'll go inside and get some ammo."

Dakota heard the car doors shut.

*All right, there are two men. And they're going to shoot me and bury me with Avner. Wow. Is this how my life is going to end, God? Buried with Avner—the guy who stole the artifacts? Please not, God. Lord, my life is in Your hands. Maybe I'll be seeing You face to face sooner than later.*

Dakota grabbed the wrench. *I might as well go down fighting.*

A couple of minutes later, he heard the men again.

"You get the ammo?"

"Yeah, here's a loaded clip. But I texted Radomir and told him we got the kid, and—"

"He's not home?"

"No. Sabiya took him to a doctor's appointment. But he texted and said he wants to meet Dakota before we kill him. He'll be home soon."

*Oh, great. This Radomir guy sounds nice.*

"Does he want us to bring Dakota inside?"

"Yeah, he said to lock him up in one of the dog cages in the workshop."

*A dog cage? Oh, brother!*

116

"All right. Let's get him out."

"Do you think he's still alive? I haven't heard a peep."

"Maybe the taser killed him—I've heard of that happening."

One of the men banged on the top of the trunk. "You in there, Dakota?"

"No," Dakota said.

One of the men laughed. "A smart aleck."

The other said, "All right, you little punk. You can come along with us peacefully, and maybe we'll spare your life, or we can put a bullet through your head. What do you want to do?"

"Peacefully works for me."

"I thought so."

The trunk popped open. The sudden flood of afternoon light was blinding. Dakota squinted. The two men grabbed him, yanked him out, and put him face down on what appeared to be a cobblestone driveway. The larger man pulled Dakota's arms behind his back and wrapped his wrists with tape.

Dakota looked around and saw the side of a large two-story white house surrounded by tall oak trees.

The men lifted him to his feet.

"Put this blanket over his head, so he can't see."

Dakota heard the trunk shut.

"All right, let's go."

Dakota felt strong hands grab his biceps and usher him off.

"Can you guys tell me what's going on? Why do you want to kill me? I haven't done anything to hurt you or—"

"You're a thief. You stole our Boss's artifact."

"Actually," Dakota said, "you guys stole it from the Israel Museum. I just found it and helped return—"

"Shut up!"

Dakota felt a blunt blow from a man's palm to the back of his head.

"Ow!" *I bit my tongue.*

The men led him up some steps and opened a door.

*I can taste blood in my mouth.* He let several drops fall inside the entryway. *Maybe detectives will be able to use that as evidence that I was here.*

*I could easily trip both men, duck down, and get this blanket off me. But then what? Get shot? My hands are taped. I'll wait for a better opportunity.*

The men escorted him through the house. Barking dogs approached Dakota.

*Sheesh—those things sound ferocious!*

Dakota lifted his right knee to keep them away.

"Do they make you a little nervous? They should."

The other man said, "Titan! Dagon! Go away. Go!"

The dogs calmed down and walked away. The men led Dakota down a hall, around a couple of corners, and unlocked a door.

"Move it . . . stop. Down to your knees!"

Dakota obeyed. *Oh, great. Is this the dog cage part?*

He heard metal sliding across the floor in front of him.

"I've got a gun to your head. I'm going to pull the blanket off, and I want you to do exactly what I tell you."

The blanket came off. Dakota quickly glanced around. *This looks like a large workshop.* On the floor was a metal cage about four feet long, three feet wide, and the same in height.

"Get in! Crawl into the cage."

Dakota felt the barrel of the gun against the back of his head. "It's hard to crawl in without the use of my hands. Could you cut the tape and—"

"Figure it out!"

One of the men kicked the backside of Dakota's right knee and sent him to the wood-plank floor. From there, he inched into the cage and onto a thin, light brown pad.

*This pad smells gross! And the dog hair . . . disgusting.*

The nausea he had in the car trunk came rushing back. *I think I'm gonna throw up. . . . Don't! That will make it worse.*

One of the men put a lock on the cage door. The other man threw the blanket over it.

"Enjoy your cage, little puppy!"

"Woof, woof!"

The men left the room laughing.

# Chapter 20

*Locked in a dark stinky dog cage?—God, this sucks. What should I do? Is there a way to get this tape off my wrists? I wonder if there's a sharp edge anywhere in the cage that I can use to cut the tape.*

After inching around the cage for several minutes, Dakota felt a little nick in the metal. *That might work.* He rubbed the tape on his wrists back and forth against the tiny sharp metal barb hoping to tear it. But a voice in the hallway outside the room interrupted the effort.

"Ah, the hooligan from California. I finally have the privilege of meeting him face to face."

Dakota heard the door open. A few seconds later, somebody pulled up the blanket covering the cage. Dakota looked

N

Marble
pedestals

Dog cage

Workshop

Roman
Empire
Hall

Wood

Paintings

Bathroom

Radomir's
Office
& Bedroom

up. A portly, pale, bald man who looked to be in his sixties was towering above the cage. From Dakota's vantage point, he looked about eight feet tall. He wore a navy suit without a tie, a white shirt, and brown oxford dress shoes. In his right hand was a dark cherry wood cane, and in his left, a gray felt hat with a narrow-curled brim.

Dakota recognized him. *That's the rude man Afton and I ran into on the boat dock in Israel! And that's the hat I pulled out of the water for him. Whoa.*

The man tapped the cage with his shoe. "What do we have here? Did my men put you in this cage? Shame on them."

Dakota didn't answer. Now that the blanket was off the cage, he scanned the room for anything he could use to help him escape. The **workshop** appeared to be about forty feet long and twenty feet wide. It had three windows with white shutters evenly spaced on one of the longer walls. A wood workbench and cabinets ran about half the length of another wall. At the far end of the room, near a door that led to a bathroom, Dakota saw a couple of sheets of plywood and other pieces of lumber. Closer to him was an old green couch, a couple of wood crates, some chairs, bar stools, and end tables.

The man said, "You're so shaken up, you can't talk. Poor thing. This cage is so inhumane. My apologies to you, Dakota Knox." He turned around and yelled, "Eeman! Bring me the key to the cage."

A minute later, Eeman walked in with the key.

"Are his hands secured?" the man asked.

"Yes."

"Unlock it for me and help him out."

Eeman unlocked and opened the door. "Get out!"

The man put his hat on and brought a stool over. "Here. Sit here, Dakota. Get comfortable."

Dakota sat on the stool facing the man.

"You're probably wondering why we've come after you."

"I think I—"

"Silence!" the man yelled. "I will tell you when you can speak. We went to great trouble and expense to relocate the Tel Dan Stele to a place where it would be properly cared for and cherished. And it was in our hands. It was on its way back here to England until—"

The man stopped, clearly agitated.

"It was on its way back here until *you* stole it from us. And then you had the audacity to do a press conference and humiliate me and my men. Did you think that was fun, Dakota?"

"I wouldn't say it was *fun*. And I wasn't trying to humiliate—"

The man lifted his cane and whacked the left side of Dakota's head. Dakota fell off the stool to his right.

"Did you like the reward money, Dakota?"

The man walked over and struck Dakota's left shin.

"Ow! . . . I turned down the reward money." Dakota tried scooting away from the man. But he followed him, swinging his cane over and over.

"You stole the David Inscription, and now you're here trying to steal the others, you fame-seeking money-mongering weasel!"

"Ow! Actually, I came to England to—"

"Well, your plans didn't go the way you hoped, did they?"

"Ow. Stop! Please, have mercy."

"Your trail ends here, Dakota! I hope your twenty minutes of fame was worth it."

"I'm not a thief . . . Ow! . . . I don't want to be famous . . . Someone help me!"

With his hands taped behind his back, Dakota was losing the fight. He tried to get away from the man without success. He blocked some cane blows with his shoes and managed to land a few kicks on the man's legs. But the man landed a dozen or more hits to his shoulders, legs, thighs, back, arms, hands, and head. Dakota's face and back were bleeding. His ears were ringing.

The man's face was red with rage when he let up. Out of breath, he said, "Had enough?"

Dakota didn't respond.

The man pulled out a white handkerchief and wiped the sweat off his forehead. He picked up his hat and walked toward the door. "Eeman, lock him back up!"

Dakota's heart was pounding.

"Would you like me to take him outside and shoot him?"

"No. Just lock him up for now. I need to extract some information from him first."

Eeman pulled out his gun. "Get back in the cage."

Dakota scooted his body over to the cage and back inside. Eeman locked it, threw the blanket over it, and walked out.

Dakota laid his head down on the hairy dog pad, closed his eyes, and broke down. *I'm in so much pain, Lord. You've got to help me. I think I'm going to die. My whole body hurts. I'm bleeding. I'm thirsty. I'm super uncomfortable with my hands behind my back. How am I going to get through this?*

As he contemplated his trying circumstances, he remembered that the apostle Paul and others had endured stonings, floggings, imprisonments, shipwrecks, and more for the sake of the gospel. *And they lived to tell about it.*

*That's it, God. I'm not giving up. I trust that You have a plan and will work everything together for good. I don't know what the plan is. It might involve me going to Heaven. But I can do all things through Christ who strengthens me. So, strengthen me, guide me, help me to escape.*

He remembered the sharp metal barb in the cage a few minutes later.

*I'm getting this lame tape off right now.*

Dakota vigorously began rubbing the tape back and forth on the nick in the metal.

*Hold on. Is that my wallet in my pocket? It is. The men didn't take my wallet—stoked!*

Dakota slid some fingers into his back pocket and pulled out his wallet. He felt for the steel multi-tool card inside and wiggled it out. With only a little difficulty, he was able to use the card's sharp blade and serrated saw to cut through the layers of sticky duct tape.

*Hallelujah! My hands are free. Thank You, Jesus.*

He pulled the blanket that was covering the cage inward to himself. *Well! That's better. I can see out now, and I can make this into a pillow and keep my head off this nasty dog pad. Thank You, God. And if it gets cold tonight, I'll have a blanket.*

He laid his head down and looked at his hands, marveling that he could hold them to his face. He decided to leave the duct tape on his wrists. Pulling it away from the hair on his wrists would be excruciating, and he couldn't bear the thought of any more pain.

Dakota looked around the room. *It seems like there are a few hours of light left. I bet if I lean against the edge of the cage and shift my weight, I can tip it over, and if I do that over and over, I could move around the room a bit. I'll do that when I have more energy. . . . I'm so exhausted. I'll just close my eyes for a little while and rest.*

# Chapter 21
## Thursday evening, June 23, Marylebone.

Back in London, the Knoxes and Hansleys were sitting in the living room of the Knoxes' apartment, talking and anxiously waiting for Dakota to come home.

"Dakota told Afton he was okay in his text," Abigail said, "but he's not answering his phone. The police haven't seen him. This isn't like him at all. I'm very concerned."

There was a knock on the door.

"Maybe it's him!" Jalynn said.

Abigail looked out the peephole. "It's two police officers." She opened the door.

"Are you Mrs. Knox?"

"Yes."

"We have an update on your son, Dakota."

"Did you find him? Is he okay? Come in."

The officers informed her that Dakota had been kidnapped. Doorbell cam footage and other findings revealed he was tasered, placed inside the trunk of a stolen silver Lexus, and driven off.

Abigail fell to the floor and cried.

The bad news sucked the oxygen out of the room—the Knoxes and Hansleys were traumatized. Tears flowed, and questions flew.

The officers assured them that several detectives were working on the case and that a countrywide child-abduction alert had been sent to people's phones.

Afton looked at her phone to see if she had received the text. She had. It had a description of Dakota and the stolen car.

When the police left, the Knoxes and Hansleys prayed, made phone calls, and strategized about what to do to help find Dakota.

Nicola reviewed the plan. "Afton, you'll get the news out on social media. Jalynn, Hank, Ethan, and Evelyn will make posters. I'll call people at our church and ask them to pray and organize volunteers to put up posters tomorrow. And Abigail, you'll call news stations."

Later that evening, after Afton informed her social media friends of the kidnapping, she leaned back against a stack of pillows propped up against her headboard. As she thought through all that transpired, Afton pieced together some things she hadn't thought of.

*If Dakota was tasered and kidnapped just a couple of minutes after we were separated, he would not have texted me and said he was "okay." Getting thrown in a trunk is not okay. He would have said that he had been kidnapped and described the vehicle or details that would help the police find him. So, that means his text was . . . a lie! Either he was forced to type it, or someone else typed it. And if that's the case, that means he's not "done" with me. He had just told me on the boat how much he loved me.*

*What a relief! . . . sort of. They might kill him, and that would be so heartbreaking. But if they* don't *kill him, if he can survive, if the police can rescue him, we will still be girlfriend and*

126

*boyfriend.*

Her heart soared.

*Oh, Lord, what else can I do to help Dakota? Guide me. I'm so glad You know where he's at, and I'm thankful You'll never leave or forsake him. I pray You'll send an angel to protect him. Peter was imprisoned in the Book of Acts and even locked up, and an angel came to him at night. The chains fell off his hands, and he walked out of prison. You can do that kind of stuff, Father! So I pray You will.*

She looked over at a photo of her and Dakota on her nightstand. It was the picture someone took of them at The Shard. She had printed it that morning and put it in a frame.

Afton rearranged her pillows, pulled the blankets up, turned off the light, and tried to fall asleep.

An hour later, she was still awake.

*I can't stop thinking about Dakota. Someone tried to kill him in Israel. So we came to England to get away from that. And now he's kidnapped? It has to be related. But how? We thought the thieves lived in Israel. Maybe they don't. Or maybe they do and they tracked us here.*

Afton whipped the blankets off, got up, and walked to the front door to make sure it was locked. It was.

She fluffed her pillow and laid back down. *Maybe that Mrs. Haddad lady on the flight was spying on us. But why would the criminals want to kill Dakota now? They would know that he doesn't have the David Inscription anymore. It's back at the Israel Museum. Its return was all over the news, so they'd know that. They must think Dakota poses a threat to them. They must think Dakota is trying to track down the other missing artifacts, and they want to stop him from doing that.*

*And if they were going to kill him in Israel, they're probably going to try to kill—I can't think that way. God, Dakota is in Your hands. Keep him safe. Maybe he's already in Your presence. I don't know. Lord, I can hardly pray. I love You. Help me to sleep. I'm so tired.*

# Chapter 22
## Thursday, June 23, Haslemere, 11:22 p.m.

The sound of the deadbolt lock on the door woke Dakota. He opened his eyes. *Is Radomir coming back to unleash more of his anger?*

The door to the workshop slowly opened. The hall light was off, so Dakota couldn't determine if the shadow was Radomir. A hand began to reach around for the light switch.

"There it is."

*That's a woman's voice.*

The lights underneath the cabinets above the workbench came on. They weren't bright enough to light up the room, but there was enough light for Dakota to see a tall woman walk by the cage toward the other end of the room. She looked Middle Eastern, maybe in her twenties, with black hair that hung halfway down her back.

Dakota stayed motionless inside the dog cage. He glanced at his watch: 11:22 p.m. *Oh wow, that was a long nap.*

The woman walked into the bathroom and turned the light on. "Ah, there's one."

The light went off, and the woman walked back toward the door with a plunger in her hand.

"Oh, my God!" she blurted out, seeing Dakota curled up in the cage. She raised the plunger next to her shoulder like a sword.

"Shh . . . Don't be startled," Dakota said. "I can't hurt you. I'm locked up in a cage."

"Eeman!" the woman yelled.

"Hey, listen—"

"Ahmed!"

"No, shh . . . please! I need your help. Two men abduck, abducked me—I'm sorry—I can hardly talk. I'm so thirsty. My mouth is supe . . . super dry." Dakota licked his lips. "Two men abducted me earlier today and locked me in this cage. I'm 17. I haven't done anything wrong. You've got to help me. They're planning to kill me."

"You sound like an American."

"I am! Two men with guns chased my girlfriend and me today in London. I think one of them is named Eeman. And—"

"Eeman is my brother."

"They tasered me, threw me in a car trunk, and drove me here. Their boss, Radomir, is going to kill me. Would you be willing to help me escape?"

The woman looked at the open door and lowered her voice. "What did you do? Why is he so mad at you?"

"I found an archaeological artifact that he stole and returned it to the museum. And now he thinks I'm in England trying to track down the other stolen artifacts. But I'm not. We came here for a family getaway just to have fun. You've got to believe me."

She walked to the door and quietly shut it. "You are telling me the truth—this I know. I heard Eeman and Ahmed talking about this, and they *do* think you're here to get the other artifacts."

"I'm not at all. My parents and I thought the thieves lived in Israel. We came here to get away from them and—"

"They *were* in Israel recently, but they live here," the woman said.

"Where is here? What town am I in?"

"Haslemere, England. Radomir is our boss." She walked closer to the cage. "You are all bruised, and your face has blood on it."

"Radomir beat me with his cane a few hours ago. My hands were taped behind my back. I couldn't fight back. Can you help me get out of this cage? I'll run out the door and be off, never to bother you again."

"What's your name?"

"Dakota Knox. Yours?"

"Sabiya."

"That's a pretty name."

"Thank you. It's Arabic. Eeman and I are from Iraq. Where are you from in the U.S.?"

"California."

"Where Hollywood is!"

"Yeah." *Unfortunately.*

"I'd like to help you, but I can't. If I help you escape, Radomir will kill me."

"Yeah, I can imagine him doing that. He's crazy."

"Yes. He's killed several people who've worked for him. Chester, the man who used to work in this workshop repairing things, making cabinets—dead."

"Radomir killed him?"

"Yep. My brother had to bury him."

"Wow. That's sad. Why'd he kill him?"

"I don't know. He's a monster. I didn't know that when I came to live here. I was just happy to get out of Iraq and away from the Taliban. I wanted to live in a peaceful home, work on my English, and have a job and freedom. But Radomir is very temperamental. One act of betrayal means death."

"Why do you stay here?"

"I have no friends or family in England, and I'm afraid of being deported if I try to get a job somewhere else."

"I understand your predicament, Sabiya, and why you can't help me. I will be praying for you. If I escape I'd love to help you find a better place to live and work. Maybe you could at least bring me some water. Maybe some food?"

"Hmm . . . I can do that. But you can't leave any crumbs or clues behind."

"Promise."

"I'll be right back."

Sabiya walked out of the room and returned a couple of minutes later. She shut the door and pulled a plastic bottle of water out of a pocket in her red plaid pajama pants. From the other pocket, she pulled out an orange.

"You're an angel, Sabiya. Thank You."

"How are we going to get this water into your mouth? I can't fit the bottle through the openings in the cage."

"A straw would work."

"I don't think we have any straws."

"Okay. I'll tilt my head back and open my mouth, and you can just pour it in."

"You trust me?"

"Well, yeah. It's not like if you miss and the water gets on me that I'll shrivel up and die." Dakota contorted his face and pretended to shrivel up.

Sabiya laughed. "Okay, tilt your head back . . . I can do that . . . More?"

"The whole bottle."

"You *are* thirsty."

After Dakota polished off all 16.9 ounces of the water, Sabiya peeled the orange and handed him individual orange slices.

"Those might be the best orange slices I've ever had, Sabiya. Thank you."

"You're welcome."

"I have some more cleaning to do. I'm Radomir's maid. When he goes to sleep around one a.m., I'll try to come back with more food for you."

"That would be amazing. And more water, please."

"More water, yes. Will you be awake?"

"Probably. I just took a five-hour nap. If not, wake me."

"Okay, Dakota. I'll try my best."

"Thank you, Sabiya."

She walked out of the room and locked the door.

*Thank You, God, for Sabiya. That water and orange blessed me so much. Bless her in return. I think of the woman who hid the Jewish spies in Jericho in the Book of Joshua. You rewarded her for her kindness. Reward Sabiya.*

# Chapter 23

Dakota adjusted his body, trying to get comfortable in the three-foot-wide cage. He looked at his watch: 1:10 a.m.

*Sabiya said she'd try to come back sometime after one o'clock with more food and water. I hope she does—I'm hungry and thirsty. God, if she's not going to help me get out of this cage, what should I do? Maybe it's not Your will yet for me to be free. You allowed this. Could good come from my captivity? Am I really going to die here in England? I didn't get to say goodbye to my family. That makes me sad. They're probably having a hard time sleeping tonight. Bless them, comfort them. If I die here, assure them I'm in Heaven and that all is well with me.*

Shortly after two a.m., Dakota concluded Sabiya wasn't coming back to help him.

*Maybe she changed her mind or fell asleep. Maybe Radomir discovered the missing orange and killed her.*

His heart sunk. He was looking forward to some nourishment and something to wet his parched tongue. As Dakota repositioned himself in the cage, he remembered Paul and Silas's beatings and imprisonment in the Book of Acts.

*They were beaten with rods and thrown into prison. I feel like I'm living through that a little bit. What did they do, God? Luke said that about midnight Paul and Silas sang songs of praise to You, and there was a great earthquake, and chains were unfastened.*

*Wow, Lord. I'm going to do that! Not so You'll send an earth-*

*quake—I don't even know if England gets earthquakes like we do in So Cal—but just because I love You, and You are worthy of praise even in the darkest of times.*

*What song should I sing first? How about that new one I learned a few weeks ago by Phil Wickham—***A 1,000 Names***. I love that song.*

Dakota hummed the melody of the song and sang:

I call you Maker
You give life an eternal spark
I call you Healer
You can mend any broken heart
I call you Faithful Father
You finish everything You start
My soul was made to respond


I know You by a thousand names
And You deserve every single one
You've given me a million ways
to be amazed at what You've done
And I am lost in wonder at all You do
I know You by a thousand names
and I'll sing them back to You, yeah,
sing them back to you, You deserve it all


Your love is boundless,
beyond what I could dream
Your grace is patient
You're never giving up on me
I call You Bondage Breaker

'cause You're handing out the prison keys
My soul was made to be free . . .

You are Rock of Ages
You're the Great I Am
You are King forever
The beginning and the end

You are Lord and servant
You're the Son of Man
You're the Lion of Judah
You're the risen Lamb

You're the second Adam
Here to lead us home
You are Yahweh's glory
Now revealed in flesh and bone

You are Ocean Parter
You will make a way
You are Death Defeater
You have risen from the grave
You are full of mercy
You are rich in love
You are Jesus, Messiah
The one true God

I know You by a thousand names
And You deserve every single one
You've given me a million ways

to be amazed at what You've done
And I am lost in wonder at all You do
I know You by a thousand names
And I'll sing them back, I'll sing them back to You
Oh, back to You

Hallelujah, Hallelujah, Hallelujah
Sing them back to You

You are full of mercy
You're rich in love
You are Jesus, Messiah
The one true God, hallelujah
Hallelujah

When Dakota finished the song, he heard the lock on the door click open. He looked at the door. *I hope that's Sabiya . . . It is! Thank God.*

She walked in, shut the door, and locked it.

"Dakota, you're up. I'm so glad. I'll leave the light off, so no one suspects anything if they look down the hall."

"That's fine. Thank you for coming back, Sabiya."

"You're welcome. I'm going to set the food down and light this candle I brought so we can see."

"Whatever you made smells amazing, Sabiya."

Sabiya lit the candle and pulled a wood chair and crate over to the cage. "Sorry, it's so late. Radomir didn't turn off his light until one forty. And I wanted to make you a hot meal. I hope you like it. It's an Iraqi dish called Makhlama."

"Anything sounds wonderful. What's in it?"

"Eggs, ground lamb, onions, garlic, parsley, cumin, lemon, tomato sauce."

"You put all that in there for me?"

"It wasn't hard."

"Well, that's so kind of you. I'll gladly eat it."

"I also brought you more water, a small tube of antibiotic ointment for your cuts, and some Motrin for any pain you're experiencing."

"You're amazing. Thank you, Sabiya. Would you mind if I pray for the meal?"

"No. I'm not religious, but please pray. I listened to you singing before I came in. That was a beautiful song. It seems that you are a Christian?"

"Yes."

"Please pray."

"Dear God, thank You for this food and for Your lovingkindness in sending Sabiya to help me through a difficult situation. Her mercy, her kindness, is a reflection of You, God. Bless this food and her. I pray in Jesus's name. Amen."

"Water first?" Sabiya asked.

"Please."

She poured water into his mouth and began handing him forkfuls of the Makhlama through the cage.

"This is delicious, Sabiya. I've never had Iraqi food."

"I'm so glad you like it."

"Earlier, I was thinking of a woman named Rahab in the Bible who risked her life helping hide a couple of men who had spied on the wicked city of Jericho. God blessed and rewarded her for her kindness to the men."

"That's in the Bible?"

"Yeah, the Book of Joshua, chapter two. I'm going to continue asking God to bless you for the kindness you're showing me."

"Oh, thank you, Dakota. I don't believe in God anymore, but that's nice of you."

"You used to believe in Him?"

"I was raised a Muslim, but after what I witnessed in Iraq under the Taliban, I rejected Islam. I rejected Muhammad, Allah, the Quran . . . all of it."

"I get that. I reject Allah too. He doesn't even exist. Muhammad invented him."

"I believe that," Sabiya said.

"But I believe there's good evidence that the God of the Bible exists," Dakota said.

"Well, I reject *that* God too."

"I'm sad to hear that, Sabiya."

"Why?"

"Because He really *does* exist and He loves you and wants to have a relationship with you."

"You talk about him like you really know him."

"I do."

"Well, I can't see him."

"I can't either, but that doesn't mean He doesn't exist."

"Well, it seems foolish to me to believe in things you can't see."

"I don't think so. Have you ever seen your thoughts?"

"No."

"But do they really exist?"

"Yes."

"Have you ever seen gravity?

"No."

"Do you believe gravity is real?"

"Of course."

"When you see a painting, do you need to see the painter to conclude a painter exists?"

"No."

"Well, the same is true with God. You don't need to *see* God to rightly conclude He exists."

Sabiya handed Dakota another heaping forkful of the Makhlama. "What leads you to believe God exists?"

With a mouthful of food, Dakota said, "Several things, Sabiya . . . excuse me while I finish chewing. Evidence for God? How about the incredible fine-tuning of the universe, the mind-boggling complexity of living organisms, the information encoded into DNA, hundreds of fulfilled prophecies in the Bible, or the historical evidence for Jesus's life, death, and resurrection. Just for starters."

Sabiya looked at him like something he said had got her thinking.

"You don't have to look far to find evidence for God, Sabiya. You can look in the mirror. When you go to your room tonight, stand in front of the mirror. Evidence for God will be staring back at you."

"I don't understand."

"Your *body* is evidence that God exists."

Sabiya shifted in the chair. "I've never thought of my body as evidence for God."

"It is. Sabiya, think about this. Your body has 206 bones, about 700 muscles, and a heart that beats over 100,000 times a day as it pumps about 75 gallons of blood an hour through more than 60,000 miles of veins, arteries, and capillaries. The eyes you're looking through right now are composed of more than two million working parts."

Sabiya looked at Dakota wide-eyed.

"Do you think all those muscles, bones, and organs pieced themselves together and started functioning apart from a designer?"

"It's hard to believe that when you break it down like that. I didn't think about all the different working parts. Two million in my eyes?"

"Two million."

"Sabiya, consider a single cell in your body. In Charles Darwin's day, cells appeared to be little unsophisticated globs of jello, mysterious little parts of life that no one could see into. But now that we can peer into cells with electron microscopes, we see that life down at the cellular level is immeasurably more complex than Darwin ever dreamed. Linus Pauling, a Nobel Prize winner who's considered the greatest chemist of the twentieth century, said that a living cell in the human body is more complex than New York City. Have you been to New York?"

"No. I'd like to go."

"It's an enormous, complex place. There are millions of people scurrying about every direction, hundreds of skyscrapers, thousands of cars, subways everywhere, boats going up and down the river, planes landing twenty-four hours a day—very complex."

"Sounds like London."

"Yes."

"Now imagine packing that kind of complexity into a single

cell, a thousandth of an inch wide, inside your body."

"That's pretty incredible."

"And your body is made up of thousands of different *kinds* of cells totaling more than thirty-seven trillion in number. And your body makes millions of new cells every *second,* and they all work together! How do they all work together? It's the DNA in the cell. The six feet of DNA coiled up inside every one of your body's cells contains a staggering amount of information and instruction that tells each cell how to function, where to go, what to do, and so on. We've learned that DNA is like a computer program but far more advanced than any software any of the tech companies have ever created."

"Wow, Dakota."

"Do you have a computer?"

"No. Radomir won't let me have one."

"Okay, a phone?"

"No. Radomir won't let me have one of those either. He's very controlling."

"Did you have a phone in Iraq?"

"Yes, nothing fancy, but yeah."

"Well, think of all the programs you used on it. Someone had to write all the code to get those programs to work, right?"

"Of course—computer programs don't write themselves. A programmer is always involved."

"Right! Well, we believe the same is true with the programming that exists in DNA. The programming points to the work of a Programmer, an intelligent designer—God."

They talked for another hour about some of the evidence for the reliability of the Bible, including the archaeological artifacts Radomir had stolen.

"I'm pretty amazed to hear all this coming from a seventeen-year-old. You're wise beyond your years, Dakota. I am definitely reconsidering my atheism. Maybe we can talk more about this God stuff tomorrow."

"Yeah, if I'm still alive, I'd love to talk more."

Sabiya stood. "I wish I could do more to help you, Dakota. Maybe if God exists, He'll give me the courage to help you escape."

"Maybe He will. I pray that He will."

She picked up the plate, the fork, the empty water bottle, and the antibiotic ointment. "I can't leave anything behind."

"Sabiya, no matter what happens. I will never forget the kindness you've shown me tonight. The food you made was one of the best meals I've ever had. Thank you."

"You're welcome, Dakota. I'll try to sneak in again tomorrow and bring you more water and a snack."

"Thank you, Sabiya. Sleep well."

"Good night."

When Sabiya walked out, Dakota prayed for her. *Heavenly Father, thank You for Sabiya. Paul said in Philippians 1:12 that his adverse circumstances in prison worked out for the furtherance of the gospel. I pray that will be the case with my imprisonment. What if this whole thing was so that Sabiya could hear about You and be drawn into a soul-saving relationship with You? This would all be worth it. You love her. Bless her. Continue ministering to her heart and mind as she ponders what I told her. And if she chooses to help me to freedom, I pray You will bless her and keep her safe.*

# Chapter 24
## Friday morning, June 24, Hansley house.

After three hours of sleep, Afton was up. She couldn't bear the gut-wrenching thought of Dakota being out there somewhere in danger. She put on a light gray sweater and a pair of jeans and walked out to the kitchen. The house was quiet and dark.

Afton turned on the coffee maker and noticed the clock: 4:15 a.m. She sat on a stool at the kitchen counter and opened her MacBook. A few minutes later, a color laser printer was churning out a hundred missing-person signs with a picture of Dakota and the police department's phone number.

As the Keurig filled her thermos with coffee, she gathered a hammer, a box of tacks, and a roll of masking tape. She wrote a note and taped it to the refrigerator.

> *Can't sleep. I'm going to look for Dakota and put up signs.*
> *Taking the Subaru. I'll be safe. Love you all! –Afton*

As she walked outside, she glanced up at the eastern sky. The 4:44 a.m. sunrise lit the clouds with beautiful shades of purple, orange, and pink.

*Brr! Glad I wore a sweater.*

She found the family's white **Subaru Crosstrek** down the street and started the engine. She closed her eyes.

"Good morning, God. Thank You for a new day and this beautiful sunrise. You see that I can't sleep. I just can't. Dakota is out there, probably in grave danger. I want to do something to help him. Will You guide my steps today? I have this stack of missing-person signs. I don't know where to put them up. I've never done this before. Direct me. Keep me safe on the road. And be with Dakota today. Help him through the day. Protect him, I pray, in Jesus' name. Amen."

She pulled the car out and drove off.

• • •

Dakota opened his eyes. Sabiya was bending down next to the cage. In a groggy voice, he said, "Oh, hey, Sabiya. It's early."

"Shh . . . thank you for talking to me last night about God. I woke up this morning, and I think God gave me a bit of courage. Not a lot—I'm very afraid. But I think He wants me to help you. I can't explain it, Dakota. I just *know* this morning that the God you spoke of last night is real. Not the god of Islam—the God of the Bible. I had a dream last night, and in the dream, I came in here, opened a drawer, found this tool, and brought it to you."

She held up a pair of bolt cutters. Dakota could hardly believe his eyes.

She opened them and angled them into the cage.

"Please don't tell anyone I gave them to you."

"I won't. Thank you, Sabiya."

"I need to hurry out before I'm discovered. I'm going to lock the door when I walk out. I found Eeman's key to this room in his pants this morning when I was doing laundry. After I walk out, I'll slide the key under the door back to you. I don't think Eeman, Ahmed, or Radomir will be able to get back in here without the key. The door requires a key on both sides."

"That's interesting. It's a double-sided deadbolt?"

"I guess. I don't know what it's called. But they can't get in without a key. If they can't get in, they can't hurt you."

"Wow, Sabiya! Amazing."

"God will give you or me an idea for the right time to escape. The windows have bars on them, so *that* door is your only way out. But now's not a good time. They're all here. Radomir has security cameras all over the property and two roaming **Rottweilers** inside the house that are trained to kill. So, it's going to be tricky."

"Okay, that's good to know."

"Two days ago, the dogs killed a man who came here from Israel to start working for Radomir."

"Yikes. He was from Israel?"

"Yeah, he worked at a museum in Jerusalem and helped Radomir with a heist. The dogs attacked him. It was awful."

"Was his name Avner?"

"Yes."

Hearing of Avner's demise put a lump in Dakota's throat. The possibility of his own death seemed even more real.

145

"Did you know Avner, Dakota?"

"Not really. But Sabiya, thank you for your help."

"You're welcome. I also hid a bottle of water and a banana in the workbench cabinet. You'll find those when you get out of the cage. And when the men are asleep or if there's another time when it's safe, I'll try to sneak in some more food."

"You're amazing, Sabiya. How are you going to get in? Should I listen for a secret knock?"

"No. I have my own key."

"Oh, okay."

"I must go now." She smiled, gently touched the top of his head through the cage, and walked out.

Dakota heard the deadbolt lock and saw Eeman's key slide under the door.

*God, this is amazing. Thank You! Bless Sabiya.*

He cut through several of the cage's steel bars, pushed off the top, and slowly stood to his feet.
*Ouch. I'm stiff and sore. But it feels so good to stand!*

• • •

After nine hours of driving around London and several surrounding towns, all of Afton's missing-person signs were up.

As Afton continued to drive around looking for the stolen silver Lexus, the futility of finding Dakota apart from a

146

miracle crashed down on her. *I haven't seen any silver Lexuses today. There are sixty-seven million people in this country, nine million in London. What am I doing? What are the chances?*

She called Madeline at the police department, hoping someone had called in with a promising lead.

"No. No promising leads yet, sweetie. But our detectives are working hard to find him."

"Thank you." Afton's heart sank.

She drove back to the street where Dakota was kidnapped. She knocked on doors, showed people Dakota's picture, and asked if they had seen anything that might be helpful to the investigation. Most people had not been home when Dakota was tasered, and those who were home hadn't seen anything unusual.

Afton walked back to the Crosstrek, sat down, and let out a long breath. She started the engine and turned on the radio. A song she had never heard came on. She looked at the screen on the dash. The song was **"Find You Here"** by Ellie Holcomb. Afton turned it up and listened to the lyrics. The first two lines broke open a well of tears.

It's not the news that any of us hoped that we would hear
It's not the road we would have chosen, no

Afton thought, *it's not!*

The only thing that we can see is darkness up ahead

*That's all I see.*

But You're asking us to lay our worry down
and sing a song instead

And I didn't know I'd find You here,
in the middle of my deepest fear
But You were drawing near,
You were overwhelming me with peace
So I lift my voice and sing:
"You're gonna carry us through everything!"
You were drawing near,
You're overwhelming all my fears with peace

Afton could barely see the road through her tears. She found a safe place to pull off the road, opened the sunroof, and extended her hands to the sky in worship.

You say that I should come to you with everything I need

*I'm here, Lord.*

You're asking me to thank You even when the pain is deep

*Thank You, God.*

You promise that You'll come
and meet us on the road ahead
And no matter what the fear says,
You give me a reason to be glad

And I didn't know I'd find You here,

in the middle of my deepest fear
But You were drawing near me,
You were overwhelming me with peace

So I lift my voice and sing:
"You're gonna carry me through everything."
You were drawing near,
You're overwhelming all my fear

Here in the middle of the lonely night,
Here in the middle of the losing fight
You're here in the middle of the deep regret,
Here when the healing hasn't happened yet

Here in the middle of the desert place,
Here in the middle when I cannot see Your face
Here in the middle with Your outstretched arms,
You can see my pain and it breaks Your heart

And I didn't know I'd find You here,
in the middle of my deepest fear
But You were drawing near,
You were overwhelming me with peace

So I lift my voice and sing:
"You're gonna carry me through everything!"
You draw near,
You're overwhelming all my fears with peace

Rejoice, rejoice!

Don't have to worry about a single thing
'Cause You are overwhelming me with peace
Don't have to worry about a single thing!
You're gonna carry us through everything
Overwhelming peace

*Oh, my goodness, Lord. I really needed that song. Bless Ellie Holcomb! I'm downloading her album. That song so ministered to my heart. I don't have to worry about a single thing. You're going to carry me through everything.*

She turned the car back on and continued toward home, feeling like someone had lifted an enormous load off her shoulders.

# Chapter 25
## Friday, June 24, Radomir's Estate, 2:37 p.m.

Radomir finished his tuna and mayo sandwich, licked his fingers, and pushed a button on the phone sitting on his desk. "Ahmed and Eeman. Come to my office."

The two men reported to Radomir and sat on the brown leather couch in front of his desk.

"I'm going to the workshop to question Dakota now. I want you two to go in there with me. When I'm done, take him outside and kill him."

"We can do that," Ahmed said.

Radomir pushed his chair back and stood. "Who has the key?"

Eeman lifted his hand. "I do." He reached into his pocket.

150

"Uh, hold on, I must have left it on my desk."

Five minutes later, Eeman walked back into Radomir's office. "Boss, I can't find the key. I had it yester—"

"Surely, we have another one."

"Uh . . . we might. I don't know where that one is either."

"When did you have the key last?" Ahmed asked.

"When we locked Dakota up yesterday. I locked the door when we walked out."

"You checked your pockets?"

"Yeah."

"Did you ask Sabiya? Maybe she found it."

"She said she hasn't seen it."

"I don't know why I allow you guys to work for me!" Radomir slammed his chair against his desk. "I'll go question Dakota through the door. Ahmed, call the locksmith—I want a new key as soon as possible. Eeman, come with me."

Radomir and Eeman walked down the hall, around the corner, and to the workshop door. Radomir tried to open it, but it was locked. He pounded on it with his fist.

"Dakota, are you in there?"

"Is someone knocking?" Dakota said.

"Yes! This is Radomir."

"Come in."

"I have a couple of questions for you. If you'll cooperate—"

"Open the door."

"If you'll answer them forthrightly, I'll set you free and let you go home."

Eeman said, "But I thought—"

"Shh!"

"Why aren't you coming in?" Dakota asked.

"Well, uh . . . um . . . there's a virus going around and—"

"There is?" Eeman asked.

"Shut up! Dakota, I just want to know *what* you know about the other missing artifacts and *who* you're working with. The Israeli government, the U.S. government, or the British?"

"None."

"Liar!"

"I'm seventeen years old. There's no way a—"

"Exactly! There's no way a teenager could track down the David Inscription and follow us to England apart from help. So, I just want to know, who is it? Who's helping you?"

"Think what you want, Radomir. I didn't have any government help."

"You maggot! You're lying! And you're going to regret it, Dakota Knox. If you thought the beating I gave you the other day was bad, wait until we get this door open!" Radomir walked away and yelled, "Ahmed! When's the locksmith going to be here?"

"Well, unfortunately, the soonest he can be here is tomorrow around 2 p.m."

"I want the two of you to look for the lost key. Tear the house apart if you must."

"Boss," Eeman said, "I think the other key might have been in Chester's pocket when we buried him."

Ahmed glared at Eeman with a facial expression that said, *I'm so disappointed you just said that.*

"Then you and Ahmed will have to dig him up."

# Chapter 26
## Friday afternoon, June 24, Radomir's workshop.

Dakota was thankful to be out of the cage and move about in the workshop. But time was ticking. The locksmith would be over the next day or sooner if Ahmed could find one who could make a house call on a Friday afternoon. So Dakota intended to escape as soon as possible. But he also agreed with Sabiya that now was *not* the time to try to sneak past three armed men and two Rottweilers. It was too risky.

As Dakota monitored the situation by listening at the door and peeking out the shutters to the front yard, he searched every cabinet and drawer for potential weapons. And there were some: a hammer, a monkey wrench, screwdrivers, a circular saw, a mallet, a box of nails, and a pocketful of nuts and bolts. *None of these is a match for a gun, but they're better than nothing.*

He laid them in strategic locations in case he was caught by surprise and needed to grab something. He also arranged the sheets of plywood, unfinished cabinets, and old furniture to create hiding places to duck behind.

*Hmm . . . what's this?* Dakota wondered as he looked out the shutters.

Radomir was getting into a dark blue Range Rover in the driveway. Sabiya was the driver. As they began to pull away, she glanced over to the windows of the workshop. Dakota backed away, not wanting Radomir to see him.

*Radomir's gone!*

A few minutes later, he heard Radomir's men talking outside. He hurried to the window to look. One of them had a shovel, and the other was holding a leash connected to two big black and brown Rottweilers. As they walked past the workshop windows, Dakota heard one of the men say, "I can't believe you buried Chester with his keys."

*Oh, wow. They're going to dig up Chester. Creepy. I'm so thankful Sabiya has the key. God, keep that key from getting into their hands!*

The men disappeared out of view.

*Now's the time—thank You, God!*

Dakota grabbed the hammer, hustled to the door, and listened for noise in the hall.

Silence.

He reached for the key in his pocket, turned the deadbolt, and quietly cracked the door. He walked into the hall. The flooring was the same as in the workshop—solid wood planks. The walls were white and lined with large oil paintings that looked hundreds of years old.

Dakota walked quickly down the hall, turned right, and passed two closed doors on his left. He turned left and walked down another hallway.

On his left, through an open door, he saw a large room that looked like a museum exhibit hall. He poked his head in for a quick peek. Across the room, on top of marble pedestals, were ancient sculptures of men and women, ceramic bowls, weapons, and other archaeological artifacts.

*And there's the stolen Pontius Pilate inscription! Radomir already has it lit up and on display. Wow.*

The shelves and cabinets along the walls had countless pieces of pottery, coins, and other artifacts. *What a collection!*

*I wonder how much of this stuff is stolen? Knowing Radomir, a lot of it.*

He wanted to look longer so he could describe what he saw to authorities, but there was no time to spare. He continued walking. The house was enormous and beautifully furnished.

*Where's the front door? This place is like a maze. Here's the kitchen. Where does this door lead? Maybe outside?* He opened the door. It was a massive garage.

Dakota took a couple of steps inside and turned on the lights. *Sheesh—How many cars does this guy own? A red Ferrari, an orange Lamborghini, BMWs, a Maserati. Crazy. But I don't have time to look.* He turned around to go back into the kitchen. On his right, he saw a rack on the wall with a dozen car keys and a landline phone.

*Oh, my goodness! I should get a call out and describe where I'm at.*

He dialed 9-1-1. *Why isn't it ringing? I thought the U.K. had 9-1-1 service. No?*

He tried again.

*Does this phone work? There's a dial tone. No answer. Ugh.*

He hung up and dialed Afton's number.

*It's ringing . . . and voicemail. Shoot!*

He tried again.

*Come on, girl! Answer . . . bummer. I'll leave a message:*

> **Dakota:** "Hey, Afton. I was really hoping you'd pick up. It's Dakota! I'm still alive. I'm being held in a white mansion on a hill by the guys who stole the artifacts in Israel. Crazy, I know. We thought they lived in Israel. But they have a house here in . . . uh, shoot, I forget the

name—it starts with an H. It's in England. I was in the trunk of a car for maybe an hour. Let the police know that the house has lots of oak trees and land around it, so there are no neighbors that I can see out the window. The mansion I'm in is two stories tall. It has several large white columns on the porch. It looks sort of like the British Museum, actually. The room I was being held in is on the first floor, northeast side. The room has black bars on the window. There's a circular driveway out front. The two men who chased us are named Ahmed and Eeman. They're away from the house, so I'm about to make a run for it, but I saw this phone in the garage and wanted to get a call out first in case they catch me trying to get away. It's a long way from the house to the street, and there are security cameras and dogs. Let the police know. Oh, no! The garage door is opening. Gotta run! I really miss you, Afton. I love you so much! Thanks for helping me. Pray for me."

Dakota hung up the phone and hurried back into the kitchen. He grabbed an orange from a fruit bowl and jammed it into his back pocket.

*And a knife rack! I think I'll take this one—thank you very much. It's a better weapon than this hammer.*

He darted around a corner and halfway down a hall. *Where should I go? Who came home? Is the person coming in through the kitchen door or the front door? Where is the front door?*

He heard the door in the kitchen open.

"All right, get back in there," a man said. "Go to your room! Radomir can walk you some other time. You guys are out of control."

*The dogs!*

Dakota could hear their claws on the floor as they walked through the kitchen. He slowly backed up. *I definitely don't want a run-in with those dogs.*

As he made his way backward with the hammer in his right hand and the knife in his left, he bumped into a framed painting on the wall.

*Shoot!*

He heard the dogs quicken their pace through the house. Within seconds, both dogs walked around the corner at the end of the hallway. With strands of drool hanging from their mouths, they locked their dark brown eyes on Dakota.

*Oh, my goodness. Those things must weigh over a hundred pounds each.*

The Rottweiler on the left tilted his head with a curious look as if to ask, *where did this delicious piece of meat come from?* The one on the right growled with a look that said, *how dare this intruder think he can wander around my castle.*

The dogs bounded toward Dakota. He hurled the hammer toward them and sprinted around the corner and back to the workshop. He pushed the door open, turned around, and slammed it shut with only a second to spare. The dogs were at the door barking like demon-possessed bloodhounds that had cornered a fox.

Dakota grabbed the key out of his pocket and locked the door.

*Whoa. That was close.*

# Chapter 27
## Friday evening, June 24, Marylebone.

Afton parked the Crosstrek in front of her home. Lack of sleep, hours of driving, and putting up missing-person signs wiped her out physically and emotionally. She leaned the seat back to rest and catch up on texts and voicemails. Several friends expressed concern about Dakota's kidnapping. She tapped on a message from a number she didn't recognize.

"Hey, Afton. I was really hoping you'd pick up. It's Dakota!

*How'd I miss your call? No!*

"I'm still alive.

*Oh, my goodness, praise God!*

"I'm being held in a white mansion on a hill by the guys who stole the artifacts in Israel. Crazy, I know. We thought they lived in Israel. But they have a house here in . . . uh, shoot, I forget the name—it starts with an H. It's in England. I was in the trunk of a car for maybe an hour.

*Oh, poor guy!*

"Let the police know that the house has lots of oak trees and land around it, so there are no neighbors that I can see out the window. The mansion I'm in is two stories tall. It has several large white columns on the porch. It looks sort of like the British Museum, actually. The room I was being held in is on the first floor, northeast side. The room has black bars on the window. There's a circular driveway out front. The two men who chased us are named Ahmed and Eeman. They're away from the house, so I'm about to make a run for it, but I saw this phone in the garage and wanted to get a call out first in case they catch me trying to get away. It's a long way from the house to the street, and there are security cameras and dogs. Let the police know. Oh, no!

*Oh, no!*

"The garage door is opening. Gotta run! I really miss you, Afton. I love you so much! Thanks for helping me. Pray for me."

*I love you too, Dakota! I'm calling 9-1-1 right now.*

Afton told the emergency dispatcher all the important details. Then she called Madeline at police headquarters. She didn't pick up, so Afton left her a message.

**Afton:** "Hi, Madeline! This is Afton Hansley. I just got a voicemail from Dakota. I missed his call. It came through about an hour ago. He's alive! He's locked up in a large white house somewhere maybe an hour outside London. I'll email you the voicemail so you can listen to all the details. Maybe you guys can track the phone number to an address. I appreciate you. Please call me back and confirm that you got the file."

Afton hung up, thankful and happy that Dakota was still alive. She got out of the car, ran to the Knoxes' rental house, and knocked on the door.

She heard Hank on the other side. "Mom! It's Afton! Can I open the door?"

"Of course."

Abigail, Hank, and Jalynn were happy to see her.

"You guys, Dakota's alive! I just got a voicemail from him. I've already called 9-1-1 and shared the file with Madeline. But come, listen."

They gathered around her phone on the couch and listened to Dakota's voice.

Abigail lifted her hands. "Praise God—he's alive!"

After listening to the voicemail a third time, Abigail said, "I need to text Dakota's dad and let him know—he's on a flight from Israel to London right now. I'm glad you sent this to the police."

"I'll send you the file right now," Afton said, "and you can forward it to him."

"Thanks. William will be so glad to hear Dak's voice. But this isn't over yet. Dakota is probably still at that house."

They prayed for him and talked for a while.

"Well, I'm going to head home," Afton said. "I'll keep you guys updated if I hear anything. Please do the same."

"Absolutely!" Abigail said.

The security guard Abigail had hired to stand in front of their door escorted Afton home. She walked into her bedroom and sat on her bed. A few minutes later, her phone chimed.

**Hank:** Hey Afton. Can you send my brother's voicemail to me too?

**Afton:** Sure.

**Hank:** I think I might be able to figure out where Dakota is. He gave us some pretty good tips. There are 3D satellite map apps and a couple of websites that will help me narrow the search.

**Afton:** Here's the VM. You're awesome Hank! I hope the police know how to use those tools too.

**Hank:** I'm sure some of the detectives do, but it's Friday night. Are they working on the case? I don't know.

**Afton:** Good question. Keep me posted. I'm going out again tomorrow morning to put more signs up. Let me know if you'd like to come.

**Hank:** Thanks for the file. Count me in for tomorrow. What time?

**Afton:** How about 7:30?

**Hank:** See you then.

# Chapter 28
## Friday evening, June 24, Radomir's Estate.

After the Rottweilers foiled Dakota's afternoon escape, he set his sights on an hour or two after midnight. Radomir and his men would be asleep, and Sabiya said the dogs like to sleep in Radomir's room.

He spent the rest of the day thinking about his escape options and planning for the possibility that the workshop was unexpectedly breached before his escape. He rearranged furniture and plywood to create momentary hiding places that might give him an advantage or buy him a few extra seconds.

*But what I really need is a better hiding place, something so good, maybe they'd think I already escaped.*

*Maybe I'll hollow out the couch and make a hiding place under the cushions. Nah, that's weak.*

*Maybe I'll cut an opening in the ceiling and hide in the air-conditioning duct like Bruce Willis did in that* Die Hard *movie. No, that's stupid. They'd see the hole in the ceiling. What else can I do?*

He continued looking and brainstorming.

*Maybe I'll make a hideout underneath the floorboards. That might work! And I have the tools to do it.*

Dakota chose a location away from the door at the southwest end of the room near the workbench. He carefully pried up a few of the wood planks from the floor. With the circular saw, he removed a rectangle section of the subflooring and a couple of floor joists. He connected the planks on the bottom sides with some small screws and thin strips of metal he found in the workbench drawers.

When Dakota was done, the planks formed a single unit that he was able to lift, move, and slide back into place on the floor. *They fit like a puzzle piece. I can't even tell there's a hideaway underneath. My woodshop teacher would be proud.*

He slid the wood planks to the side, crawled into the hideout, and laid down. Beneath him was a thick sheet of plastic on top of cold dirt. On his left was a galvanized steel pipe and what looked like a heating duct. A wood floor joint on his right ran parallel with his body.

*I fit. This works great.*

Dakota pulled the wood over him and lowered it into place. There were about five inches of clearance between the tip of his nose and the floor.

*Hopefully, I won't have to use this hiding place, but it's here if I need it.*

He pushed the wood up, got out, and cleaned up the sawdust and debris.

Dakota felt his stomach grumble. *I'm hungry again. At least I have water. I'm thankful for that.* He had plenty of water now that he was out of the cage and had access to the tap water in the bathroom sink.

At ten forty-five p.m., Dakota decided to lie on the old couch and rest for a couple of hours. He set his watch alarm for one fifteen a.m., hoping to wake up and be off and running.

# Chapter 29
## Saturday morning, June 25, Radomir's Workshop.

Dakota's alarm went off at one-fifteen a.m. He sat up on the couch, a little disoriented but thankful he had gotten a bit of sleep. He walked around the room checking on his plywood defenses, under-the-floor hideout, and improvised weapons.

*Okay, Lord, I think it's time. Radomir should be asleep soon. I pray You'll help me escape . . . that You'll lead me out of here like the angel led Peter out of prison. Thank You for Sabiya and this key. I'd be in that dreadful cage and probably dead by now from dehydration if it wasn't for her. So, bless her for risking her life and helping me. Protect her from Radomir. Lead her to another job. But more importantly, I pray for her salvation. Draw her to Yourself, God. You love her. And it's in Jesus's name, I pray. Amen.*

Dakota did some stretching and shadowboxing to wake himself up and get his blood flowing. He grabbed the knife he had taken from the kitchen, stuffed a fist full of bolts into his pocket, and exhaled a long breath. *I think I'm ready. Let's roll, Lord!*

He walked to the door and listened.

The hall was quiet.

He unlocked the door, slowly opened it, and walked down the dark hallway, feeling his way along the wall. *I'm glad I got to see the layout earlier when it was light.* He turned right at the corner and passed the two doors on his left. *I'm pretty sure those doors go into Radomir's exhibit hall.*

At the end of the hallway, he turned left and saw flickering light coming out underneath a door on the right.

*What's that? Is that Radomir's room? Is he still up? I should have asked Sabiya where his bedroom was. Should I turn around? No. Tonight's the night—I've got to get out of here! Should I run past it? No. I need to be quiet.*

He continued moving toward it.

When he was about six feet from the door, he heard a man's voice and stopped. He leaned forward and listened.

"Nebuchadnezzar, the great king of Babylon.

*That's Radomir!*

"You laid waste to inferior kingdoms and are now the most powerful ruler of all the Babylonian kings. I am Radomir, the chief commander of your mighty warriors.

*He's talking to Nebuchadnezzar? He died like twenty-six hundred years ago.*

"I will go out to battle for you! I will lead your men to victory.

*He sounds drunk.*

"We will vanquish your enemies, and I, Radomir Lucic, will expand your kingdom to the furthest corners of the world. The fear-inducing power of your authority as the king of all the Earth resides in my cane."

*His cane?*

Dakota nearly burst out laughing, but he put the brakes on inside his nose. He didn't intend to make a peep, but he did.

It was the tiniest noise.

But Rottweilers have a keen sense of hearing, especially when they've been trained to protect their master at the slightest sign of danger. And they immediately went crazy on the other side of the door.

*Oh, no! If I run forward, I might get lost in the house and mauled to death by dogs or shot. If I run back to the workshop, I escape the dogs and maybe get shot tomorrow when the locksmith shows up. Both options are terrible.*

With only a couple of seconds to weigh his options, Dakota decided to retreat. He scurried back to the workshop, shut the door, and locked it. *Ugh! My stupid laugh. I shouldn't have stopped at Radomir's room.*

He stood in the dark, listening at the workshop door. Within thirty seconds, the Rottweilers were going berserk on the other side, barking and clawing at the wood.

Dakota heard Radomir talking as he walked down the hallway. "What'd you hear, Titan? Hmm? Dagon? Did the boy make some noise in there? Is he up to something nefarious? All right, enough. Stop barking! You can have at him tomorrow."

At Radomir's command, they stopped barking. "But in case Dakota's plotting any kind of escape in there, I'll let you sleep in the hallway tonight."

Dakota laid on the couch, relieved to be safe, but frustrated that his escape had been thwarted again by those *idiotic, overgrown, demon-possessed, flea-ridden, hair-shedding, smelly dogs! I never want a dog for as long as I live!*

He tried to fall asleep, but the adrenaline rushing through his veins wouldn't let him. Half past two in the morning, Dakota heard the door unlock. He jumped off the couch, knife drawn.

"Dakota? It's me, Sabiya."

"Phew! That's a relief. Come in."

She came in and locked the door. "I have food for you. You must be starving."

"Oh, wow, you're a blessing. I *am* starving. Thank you!"

"I'm sorry I couldn't come by sooner. The men have been around all day, and Radomir was up late."

"Yeah, I know."

She lit a small candle in a glass jar and set it on the wood crate in front of the couch.

"How'd you get past the dogs, Sabiya?"

"Oh, they love me. They follow me around as I clean the house, and I give them lots of rubs."

"Wow. They *hate* me." He motioned with his hand. "Here, please, why don't we sit on the couch?"

"Thank you. So, I hope you like what I brought you," Sabiya whispered. "I took Radomir to a doctor's appointment earlier, and while I was waiting for him, I walked over to a little burger place and got you a couple of cheeseburgers."

"Are you serious? Oh, my gosh! That sounds so good."

"I warmed them up a few minutes ago." She pulled them out of a brown paper bag and set them on the crate. "I also brought you a bottle of water and a Coke."

"You're amazing, Sabiya. Wow. Thank you. I'd pay you back right now if I had any cash in my wallet."

"You don't need to pay me back—you are my friend, and I am happy to help you."

As Dakota devoured the first cheeseburger, he updated her on his thwarted attempts to escape.

"Well, the time wasn't right, I guess. God has a plan for you, Dakota."

"I believe that. Thank you."

Dakota cracked open the cold soda. "I haven't had a Coke in a long time. Thank you!"

"I thought you might like it."

"So, it was a blessing to hear you say that you believe in God, Sabiya."

"Yes, what you said last night about the human body and the archaeological evidence for the Bible really opened my eyes, and then that *dream* I had. I just woke up *knowing* God exists."

"That's so awesome. What are your thoughts about Jesus?"

"I'm not sure. You were singing to Him yesterday. I grew up learning He was a prophet of Islam."

"Hmm. Well, Jesus couldn't have been a prophet of Islam," Dakota said. "Islam wasn't even around in the first century. Muhammad invented Islam six hundred years *after* Jesus walked the Earth."

"That would be a problem, for sure. I was also taught from the Quran that Jesus was never put to death on a cross."

"Well, Muhammad was certainly mistaken about that."

"Why do you think?"

"Sabiya, there's a bunch of historical evidence that Jesus was crucified. The disciples, the eyewitnesses of Jesus's life, tell us about the crucifixion in the New Testament, but other historical sources *outside* the Bible mention it as well."

"I didn't know that."

"A lot of people don't know that. For example, Flavius Josephus, a first-century historian—he talks about it. And Cornelius Tacitus, a Roman historian—he mentions it. There's enough evidence for Jesus's crucifixion that historians consider it an indisputable fact."

"Interesting. The Quran says it never occurred."

"I know, but the Quran was written six hundred years *after* Jesus's crucifixion by men who never met Jesus and who lived more than seven hundred miles away. It's not a trustworthy record of Jesus's life."

"What I don't understand is why—*why* would Jesus have had to die?"

"Good question. Well, because God is loving and holy and just, He hates sin. Sin hurts people. It alienates us from God. It grieves our Maker. So, sinners deserve judgment, condemnation, and death. But rather than pouring all that out on you and me, God determined that He'd punish Jesus so that *we* could be freely forgiven, rescued from eternity in Hell, and brought back into a right relationship with Him."

"It's hard for me to imagine that God would treat one of His prophets that way."

"Sabiya, Jesus wasn't some random man God treated that way. Jesus was and is God."

"I heard you singing the other night. And you said Jesus was the Messiah, the one true God. Is that what Christians believe? That Jesus is God?"

"Yes. The Bible makes that clear. Jesus, God in the flesh, came to the Earth on a rescue mission to save us. He laid down

His life on the cross, Sabiya, out of love for you. Do you know that? God loves you!"

"I didn't hear God loved me much growing up in Islam."

"Well, God *does* love you, Sabiya. So much. Jesus said that 'God so loved the world that He gave His one and only unique Son, that whosoever believes in Him should not perish but have everlasting life. For God did not send His Son into the world to condemn the world, but that the world through Him might be saved.'"

"Jesus said that?"

"Yeah, He did."

"Hmm."

Dakota heard a dog walk up to the door. He lowered his voice to a whisper in case Radomir was standing outside the door. "Sabiya, I have a sneaking suspicion that God didn't allow me to escape tonight because He wanted us to have this conversation."

"I'm sorry if that's the case."

"I'm not! If that's part of His plan, I *want* that. My life is in His hands, and I want you to come to Heaven with me, Sabiya."

"How do I do that? I *do* want to go to Heaven . . . not tonight, but you know."

"Yeah, I know what you're saying. How does a person go to Heaven? Jesus said, 'whosoever *believes* in Him will not perish.' So, all you really need to do is place your faith in Him."

"That's it?"

"Yep, the Bible says salvation is a 'free gift.' And you can lay hold of it tonight. God is a prayer away."

"I'm not very good at praying."

"Would you like for me to lead you in a prayer?"

"Yes."

"If you believe what I told you, pray something like this: God, thank You for loving me. Thank You for dying on the cross for my sins, Jesus. Please forgive me. I trust in You, Jesus, to save me. Come into my life and be my Lord and Savior. And it's in Your name that I pray. Amen."

Sabiya repeated every word but then kept praying. "God, I'm not good at praying but thank You for sending Dakota here. He opened my eyes about You. I don't know if I ever would have heard the things he shared with me unless I had met him." She wiped tears off her cheeks. "You sent a light into a dark house and lit up the path for me. Thank You. I don't know Your plan for him, but please help him make it home safe. Bless him. Amen."

"Amen. Thank you, Sabiya!"

She gave Dakota a long hug. "Thank you." They talked for a bit longer about the importance of reading the Bible.

"Thank you, Dakota. I must go now, and you need to get some sleep."

"Thank you so much for the hamburgers. Such a blessing." Dakota picked up the candle and walked Sabiya to the door. "Are you sure you can walk down the hallway without the dogs barking at you?"

She smiled at him. "Watch. Actually, *don't* watch. Lock the door. But I will be fine." She walked out.

Dakota locked the door, laid on the couch, and closed his eyes. *Wow, Lord. Sabiya placed her faith in Jesus. Amazing. Bless her as she walks with You!*

# Chapter 30
## Saturday morning, June 25, Marylebone.

Afton woke up Saturday morning, read her Bible, and walked into the kitchen. Her phone chimed as she spread cream cheese on an everything bagel.

**Hank:** Hey Afton, you awake yet?

**Afton:** Yes, printing more signs right now. You still up for going this morning?

**Hank:** For sure. I've narrowed down the homes Dakota might be at to three.

**Afton:** Really!

**Hank:** Dakota said he was being held in a large white mansion on a hill in a town that starts with an H within an hour's drive of London. He said the house was two stories, had large white columns on the porch, and a circular driveway out front. There are only three homes that have all those. Each one is in a different town.

**Afton:** Okay, wow. Great work! Why don't we put signs up in those towns, and we'll drive by those houses and take a look.

**Hank:** I think that would be good.

**Afton:** Meet me outside at the white Subaru Crosstrek in ten minutes. Would you like a bagel with cream cheese?

**Hank:** Is the Pope Catholic?

**Afton:** Haha. I'll make you a bagel.

**Hank:** Thanks. Is your brother Ethan coming?

**Afton:** No. He's helping my mom with the church volunteers. Just you and me.

**Hank:** Okay. See you in ten.

Afton and Hank drove to Horsham, forty-three miles south of London, to check out the first house. They drove by the home three times. But the place was for sale and had a padlock on the gate at the foot of the driveway. The house was also more beige than white. They agreed that it couldn't be the house Dakota described. But Afton pulled the car over in a few places for Hank to put up missing-person signs.

The next house was in the town of Horley, thirteen miles northeast of Horsham.

"I think this one might be the one," Hank said.

"It's worth a look."

When they pulled off the road near the estate, Hank rolled down his window. "See the house up there, Afton? It's white. It has large columns and all the things Dakota mentioned. Big oak trees."

"Hmm. I wish I had brought our binoculars, Hank."

"I brought some I found at the house. They're in my backpack. I also brought my **drone**."

"Oh, cool!" Afton looked through the binoculars. "I think this *could* be it, Hank."

"I'll fly my drone up there and take a closer look."

A couple of minutes later, Hank's drone was in the air, zooming across the top of the oak trees towards the house. The two teens sat in the Subaru, watching Hank's phone screen to see what the drone's camera was streaming.

"Can you move it in closer?" Afton asked. "It doesn't look like anyone's home."

Hank brought the drone close enough to the house to see through an upstairs window. "I see furniture, but everything is covered with white sheets."

"That's creepy looking, and I don't like looking into someone's house. Let's back it away," Afton said. "I don't think anyone's living there. It looks like the owner covered the furniture to protect it from dust. I don't think this is the house, Hank. Dakota said some men *live* in the house."

Afton pulled out a piece of paper from her pocket. She had written down Dakota's descriptions of the house. "Hank! Dakota said the room on the northeast side had black bars on the windows. Fly the drone over there."

It was clear a minute later that there were no black bars on any of the windows.

"Sorry, Afton. I couldn't tell that from the satellite photos."

"That's okay. We can rule this house out. Let's check out the next one. Where's it at?"

"Haslemere, thirty-four miles southwest of here."

"Okay, let's put up a few signs here in Horley and head over

there."

When they arrived in Haslemere, Afton parked the Crosstrek on the side of the road near the estate's massive black iron gate. "You see it up there, Hank? It's hard to see through the trees, but it's white. And I can see the tops of a couple of the columns."

"This house has everything Dakota described," Hank said, "but I don't know about the black bars. The satellite photo wasn't that clear. I'll get the drone in the air and take a look."

Hank stood outside the car and flew the drone up toward the house.

Afton looked over his shoulder at his phone screen. *Dakota, are you in there? Is this the right house?*

Hank dropped the drone down between the oak trees and got a better view of the front of the large white house

"Oh, my goodness, Hank! Black bars on the window, northeast side."

Hank gulped.

"Fly it in closer."

Hank maneuvered the drone about twenty feet away from the house on the northeast side. "This is exactly what Dakota described."

"It is, Hank! Can you fly it around the corner?"

"Sure."

"I'd like to see if there's a door or window on the other side that might—"

"Oh, shoot, Afton. The battery on the drone is low. It's going to automatically return to me before it dies."

"That's fine. I think *this* is the house."

About a minute later, the drone landed in Hank's hand.

"That thing's amazing!" Afton said.

As the two discussed what to do next, a black Audi A8 pulled up to the gate about 30 yards from where Afton had parked. A man with a black baseball cap and silver-framed sunglasses looked at them through his window. He turned the car off, opened the door, and walked toward them with a Star-bucks cup in his left hand. "May I help you?"

Afton raised her voice as the man was still a way off. "We're looking for a missing person. His name is Dakota Knox."

Hank whispered out of the side of his mouth, "I don't know if I would have said that. He's not going to admit—"

The man stopped a few feet in front of them.

"Here's his picture," Afton said. "Have you seen him?"

"No. I don't recognize him." He reached his right hand behind his back and seemed to feel for something along his waist. He was visibly irritated that whatever it was, wasn't there.

Afton continued. "We got a phone call from Dakota, and he said he was being held in a white house with large columns in the front, surrounded by oak trees on a hill in a town that started with an H. This house checks off all those descriptions, so I'm—"

"Whoa, whoa," the man said. "Are you insinuating that me,

my wife, and kids are the ones who kidnapped the young man you're looking for?"

"No, but—"

"We are a law-abiding, loving family, highly respected in the community. We support the local foster home and would never take a young man and hold him against his will."

"I'm not *insisting* that you have him here at your house," Afton said. "It's just that your house is *exactly* like the one he described in a voicemail."

The man took a sip of his coffee. "Well, there are dozens of houses that look like ours in southern England, but I'll tell you what. I'll open the gate, and you two can follow me up the driveway, come inside our house, and take a look."

Afton looked at Hank. It was a tempting offer, but Afton knew it was never wise to go into a stranger's home. "No, thanks for offering, though."

"No, please come," the man said. "Just take a quick peek. My wife will make you some tea—and we've got cookies."

"Are they homemade?" Hank asked.

"That's very nice of you to offer," Afton said, "but that won't be necessary. We'll keep looking."

"All right," the man said, "I hope you find him. And if you'd like, please tape up one of your missing-person signs on our fence here. And we'll pray for his safe return."

"Thank you."

"What's your name?" the man inquired.

"Afton."

Hank reached out his hand. "I'm Hank."

"Omar."

"Nice to meet you, Omar."

Afton said, "Thank you, Omar. I'm sorry we've—"

She was interrupted by the noise of a white van that drove up to the gate. She looked over Omar's shoulder and read the business name on the van: Haslemere Locksmith.

Afton finished her sentence. "I'm sorry we've taken up your time, Omar. We'll be going."

"Remember to put up a sign," the man said as he turned and walked toward the van.

Afton taped a sign to the black iron fence, hopped in the Subaru, and shut the door. "It's crazy. That house seemed so close to what Dakota described."

"Totally!"

"But it's hard to imagine a kidnapper inviting us to come into his house to look around, unless . . . nah."

"And the man is married and said he'd pray for us," Hank said. "He didn't seem like a kidnapper."

Afton started the engine. "I'm going to stop at the tiny coffee shop down the road and get an iced coffee. And then we can continue putting signs up if you're up for it."

"Sure," Hank said.

When the barista handed Afton her coffee, Hank said, "They spelled your name wrong."

"That wouldn't be the first time."

"They spelled it *A-f-t-i-n*," Hank said.

Afton glanced at the cup. Seeing her name misspelled reminded her of the unusual name she had seen on the man's Starbucks cup at the house: AHMED.

"What! *Ahmed?*" Afton said out loud.

"Huh? Who's Ahmed?"

"That guy at the last house told us his name was Omar. He

was lying! I distinctly remember seeing the name *Ahmed* on his cup when we talked to him. Why would he lie to us about his name? Oh, my goodness. Get in the car, Hank! We're going back!"

They hopped in and drove off.

"Hank, play Dakota's voicemail again."

"Here it is."

> **Dakota:** "Hey, Afton. I was really hoping you'd pick up. It's Dakota! I'm still alive. I'm being held in a white mansion on a hill by the guys who stole the artifacts in Israel. Crazy, I know. We thought they lived in Israel. But they have a house here in . . . uh, shoot, I forget the name—it starts with an H. It's in England. I was in the trunk of a car for maybe an hour. Let the police know that the house has lots of oak trees and land around it, so there are no neighbors that I can see out the window. The mansion I'm in is two stories tall. It has several large white columns on the porch. It looks sort of like the British Museum, actually. The room I was being held in is on the first floor, northeast side. The room has black bars on the window. There's a circular driveway out front. The two men who chased us are named Ahmed and Eeman. They're away from the house, so I'm about to make a run for it—"

"Stop the message."

"Ahmed!" Hank said. "The very name on that man's Starbucks cup."

"Exactly. That *is* the house!" Afton pressed the gas pedal

down. "Let's see what you can do, Subaru. Hey Siri, call Madeline!"

While the phone was dialing, Afton said, "Hank, I recognize that guy now. He was one of the men who chased Dakota and me the other day. He had a hat and shades on a few minutes ago, so I didn't recognize him, but he was definitely one of the guys!"

"Oh, wow."

"Voicemail again, Madeline? Does she ever pick up her phone? . . . Hi Madeline, this is Afton. We found the house where Dakota is! The address is . . . Send police there right now, please. This is *for sure* the place. I'll call 9-1-1, as well. Thanks. Bye."

Afton told the emergency dispatcher the same thing.

The woman said, "I'll send the next available officer to look into it. Please stay away from the property. The men involved in the kidnapping were armed and dangerous."

"Oh, I *know* they were dangerous. Thanks for the advice." Afton ended the call and thought *that's precisely why we're going back—Dakota's in danger!*

"Let's pray, Hank. Father God in Heaven, we've had a bit of a breakthrough here, as You know. Please continue to watch over us. Keep us safe. If Dakota is still alive, please keep him safe. We need you. Thwart the plans of these evil men. Give us wisdom. Give us courage. Direct our steps in Jesus's name, Amen."

"Amen!"

# Chapter 31

Dakota woke up on Saturday morning and looked at his watch: 10:27 a.m.

*What! How'd I sleep in so late? Oh, yeah, I was up super late talking to Sabiya. That was awesome. All right, I have to get out of here. I heard Ahmed say in the hallway yesterday that the locksmith could come over today at two o'clock. That's in about three and a half hours.*

He walked into the bathroom, splashed water on his face, and ran some of it through his messy hair. As he swished water around his mouth, he thought, *I can't wait to brush my teeth again, take a hot shower, and put on some clean clothes.* Dakota was thankful the workshop had a bathroom, but it didn't have a shower, soap, or towels, just a sink, mirror, toilet, and a couple of rolls of toilet paper.

As Dakota dried his hands on his dirty, blood-stained tee shirt, he heard a vehicle pull up in front of the house. He walked to a window and peeked out the shutters.

*Haslemere Locksmith!* The sight of the van sent a jolt of adrenaline through his heart. *Oh, man—he's early!*

Dakota quickly grabbed the kitchen knife and mallet, lowered himself into his underfloor hiding place, and pulled the wood planks back into place. He could feel his chest pounding.

A couple of minutes later, Dakota heard men talking in the hallway.

The workshop door opened.

"Okay," Radomir said, "thank you for your service. Ahmed,

why don't you escort the locksmith back to the front door. Eeman, come with me."

"Ah, you managed to get out of the cage," Radomir said. "I must say, you're very clever, Dakota Knox. Where are you hiding, you little scumbag?"

Dakota stayed perfectly still. *God, please don't let them find me.*

"I'll check the bathroom," Eeman said.

"He's got to be in here somewhere," Radomir said. "Are the windows broken?"

"No, they're intact."

"Tear the room apart!"

Dakota heard cabinet doors slam shut and his plywood-furniture hiding places knocked over.

"Where's the kid?" Ahmed asked when he returned to the workshop.

"He's gone!" Eeman said.

"He's hiding somewhere. Did you look in the workbench cabinets?"

One of the men walked toward the workbench and stopped. Dakota could see a shoe right above his nose through the tiny crack between the planks.

Dakota expected bullets to pierce the wood flooring any second. *Oh, God, I don't want to die under here! Please.*

"Did you check under the couch cushions?" Ahmed asked.

"Didn't think of that."

The man walked away from Dakota's hiding place.

"Plug your ears, Boss."

Dakota heard five gunshots. Poom! Poom! *These guys are crazy!*

"Don't just stand there!" Ahmed said. "Yank the cushions off."

"Nothing but fabric with holes," Eeman said.

Radomir said, "Go to your house, Ahmed, and check the security camera footage. He must have got out."

"Will do."

"Eeman, take the dogs outside and search the property."

"Yes, Boss."

"That little nuisance. If Sabiya or Dario helped him escape, they'll lose their heads!"

Dakota listened to the men talk as they left the room. A couple of minutes later, he slowly pushed up the wood flooring, scanned the room, and crawled out of his hiding place. The workshop was a mess.

Radomir was yelling down the hallway.

Dakota grabbed the mallet and knife and stuffed a handful of nuts and bolts into his pocket.

*Now's the time. Radomir's men and the dogs are outside. I'll take my chances with a one-on-one encounter with that godless monster. God help me!*

He ran to the door and quickly made his way down the hall. He peeked around the corner at the first right turn. The hall was clear, and the two doors on the left were closed. Dakota hurried along the wall and eyed the next hallway. Radomir's office door was open.

*Is he in there?*

Dakota continued walking—kitchen knife in his left hand, mallet in his right.

Suddenly, the doorway darkened, and Radomir stepped into the hall fifteen feet in front of him. He turned, and appeared startled. "Oh! *There* you are! You're a shrewd young man, Dakota Knox. And soon, you'll be a dead one." He shouted, "Eeman, Ahmed! Come and kill this unshaven rat." Looking Dakota up and down, he said, "I see you've got some cuts and bruises. Don't worry. Soon you won't feel them at all."

"Out of my way," Dakota yelled, "or I'll kill you!"

Radomir laughed. "You're a Christian. The Bible says, 'you shall not murder.'"

Dakota slowly moved forward. "I guess you haven't read where Jesus told His disciples, 'If you don't have a sword, sell your cloak and buy one.' Jesus upheld our right to self-defense."

"Eeman!"

Dakota hurled the mallet at him as hard as he could. It hit him square in the chest.

Radomir grimaced in pain. "Oh, you'll regret that, Dakota. Eeman! Ahmed! Titan!"

"Looks like they're outside and can't hear you." Dakota slowly moved forward with the carving knife in his right hand. "Move out of the way!"

"Never!"

Radomir lifted his wood cane like a baseball bat.

Dakota moved in closer and swung the knife at Radomir, trying to scare him off. He lunged and jabbed—all misses. Radomir swung his cane from the right and then the left. Dakota dodged both attempts. But Radomir's next swing hit Dakota's neck. The pain was searing.

Dakota swung the knife and felt it slice Radomir's upper left arm.

Radomir hollered in pain. But his subsequent cane swing hit Dakota's right forearm and knocked the knife out of his hand. "Ha! Who taught you how to fight?" Radomir asked.

Dakota glanced down for the knife—it was several feet behind him. Radomir swung his cane again and hit Dakota's right shoulder so hard that it sent him to the ground. Dakota was on his back. He pushed himself toward the knife while Radomir swung his cane at his legs twice, both misses.

"It's a little harder now that my hands aren't taped, isn't it, Radomir?"

"Oh, Dakota, this will be over shortly." Radomir walked backward and into his office.

Dakota kept his eyes on the office door and scooted back a few more feet. He reached into his jeans, wrapped his fingers around a fist full of nuts and bolts, and grabbed the knife with his other hand. As he stood, Radomir walked out of his office with a large blood stain on his left sleeve and a black handgun in his right hand.

Radomir raised the gun and pointed it at Dakota. "Haven't you heard you're not supposed to bring a knife to a gunfight?"

"That's why I brought a bunch of these, you nutjob." Dakota hurled his fist full of metal at Radomir like he was pitching in the World Series. As the nuts and bolts flew through the air, a hollow point nine-millimeter bullet from Radomir's gun whizzed toward Dakota. The bullet went over his head, but a dozen pieces of steel pelted Radomir in the face, chest, and lower abdomen.

The pain sent Radomir backwards to the floor with a thud.

*Strike three—you're out, loser!*

Dakota ran toward him.

Radomir started to lift the gun, but Dakota stepped on his wrist, pulled the Sig Sauer 9mm pistol out of his hand, and pointed it at him. "Turn over and crawl into your office on your hands and knees, or I'll put a hot piece of lead between your eyes."

With blood dripping down his left arm, Radomir complied. When he was in the room, Dakota shut the door and said, "You open this door before the police arrive, you die. Got it?"

Dakota turned around, went into the artifact hall, and lifted the **Pontius Pilate stone** off a marble pedestal. "This is coming with me." *I'd grab more if I had time.*

He ran through the kitchen with the limestone slab under his left arm and the gun in his right hand. He opened the door to the garage, quickly scanned the key fobs hanging on the wall, and found the one with the Lamborghini logo.

*Always wanted to drive one of these.*

He hit all three garage door buttons on the wall and ran over to the orange Lamborghini. He tapped the button on the driver's side door and watched it open vertically. *That is so cool.*

Dakota sat in the driver's seat on the right side and laid the artifact in the passenger seat.

*This dashboard! Wow.*

He turned the engine on.

*Whoa! This thing's a monster. It sounds more like a growling dragon than a V–12 engine.*

The Lamborghini had been backed into the garage, so Dakota was able to drive straight out. He gave it a little gas knowing it had enough power to hit sixty miles per hour in 2.8 seconds, but it was still too much gas. He nearly hit the fountain forty yards away in the middle of the circular driveway.

*Sheesh! Careful now, Dakota.*

He backed off the grass near the fountain, turned the car onto the cobblestone driveway, and began driving down the curvy driveway.

"Woohoo! I'm free," Dakota yelled. "Thank You, God!"

As he said those words, he thought he saw two people duck behind some shrubs near the bottom of the hill. *Were those Radomir's men? The landscapers? Or was I seeing things?*

He stopped the Lamborghini at the gate and nervously waited for it to open. The gate looked like it was trying, but something was blocking it.

"Come on!" *I'm a sitting duck here.*

He looked out the left window toward the shrubs. *I hope those weren't Radomir's men. Why isn't the gate opening?*

Dakota grabbed Radomir's pistol off the passenger seat and got out of the car. He kept his eyes on the shrubs and walked over to the gears that opened and shut the gate.

"Dakota!"

He instantly recognized the voice, turned, and looked up the hill. Afton was standing there.

"Afton!"

Hank popped up a few feet away from her. "Hey, big bro!"

"Hank! Oh, my gosh, I thought you might be the bad guys. I'm so glad to see you two. I just escaped the house. We need to leave. The men who live here are super evil. They have guns and won't hesitate to shoot. But the dumb gate won't open."

"Oh! I can fix that," Hank said. "I put a big rock in the gears so the bad guys couldn't leave." Hank ran over to the gears and pulled out the rock.

Afton ran to Dakota and gave him a big hug. "Oh, Dakota,

I'm so glad you're alive. Wow. I love you!"

"I love you so much, Afton. I missed you like crazy! But we have to get out of here, like right now. Hurry, Hank! Get in, guys."

Dakota slid the gun into his back pocket and placed the Pontius Pilate slab behind the passenger seat.

Hank and Afton shared the empty seat.

Dakota pushed a button, and the Lamborghini's doors lowered. "The gate opened! Thanks, Hank. We're out of here." He turned right and punched the gas.

"Yesss—this thing's a beast!" Hank exclaimed.

"Switch lanes!" Afton said. "You're driving on the wrong side of the road."

"Yikes. I forgot."

"Dakota, you've got bruises on your arms and neck and a cut on your head."

"Yeah, I took a bit of a beating. I'll be okay. I have no idea where we are. Can you find the closest police station on your phone? We'll drive straight there."

After a few taps on her phone, Afton started giving Dakota directions.

"Can't believe we're driving in a **Lamborghini**," Hank said. "These things can go over three hundred miles per hour!"

"Yeah, straight to the hospital or jail," Dakota said.

As they drove along the rural two-lane road, Dakota told them about some things that happened. Afton updated him on what they had been doing to find him. She also texted their moms, informing them that Dakota was safe and on his way to a police station.

"See that poster on the fence with your cute face?" Afton

said.

"Oh, wow, missing-person posters?"

"Yeah, hundreds all over London and the surrounding towns."

"Never thought I'd end up on one of those."

"A lot of people are concerned and praying for you, Dakota . . . Here's the police station. Turn in right here."

Dakota pulled the Lamborghini into the parking lot.

"I wonder why the parking lot is empty. It looks closed," Afton said.

Dakota parked the car. "Well, it's Saturday. And officers usually park their cars in a gated area around the back."

The three teens got out and walked toward the entrance. Afton put her arm around Dakota's side. He knocked on the glass door and looked through the window.

No answer.

"Maybe my map app needs to be updated," Afton said.

"All right, back to the car. We'll find a station that's open."

As they turned to walk back to the car, Afton said, "What's that noise?"

"That looks like a drone," Hank said. "A big one!"

Dakota looked up. Hovering about a hundred- and fifty-feet overhead was a black octagon-shaped drone that looked about five feet wide with several angled edges. Above the drone's body were six propellers, one at each end of six arms that extended a couple of feet from the drone. The arms each had small blinking red lights on their tips.

"Oh my goodness, that's Radomir's drone!" Dakota said. "Get in!" They hopped in the car and lowered the doors. The tires screeched as Dakota pulled out of the empty parking lot.

"Hold on!"

In his side mirror, Dakota saw a slew of bullets coming from the drone and chewing up the pavement behind the Lamborghini. "The drone is following us and firing at us! Buckle up!" He gave the car more gas and swerved to avoid the gunfire. "That's got to be Radomir's drone."

"Who's Radomir?" Hank asked.

"He's the evil mastermind behind the heist at the museum and who's trying to kill me. That's the drone they used to airlift the artifacts and blow up that building. Call the police, Afton. Have them direct us to a police station that's open, and I'll try to lose that thing."

Hank leaned over and looked at the speedometer. "Whoa, Dak, we're going over a hundred miles an hour!"

"It's either that or a fiery death when a bullet punctures the gas tank."

Afton had the police dispatcher on the phone. "Okay, Dakota, you need to make a right coming up here."

"I can't make that turn. We're going too fast! Shoot. My fault."

Hank said, "There's a bridge up there, Dak. Stop underneath. We'll have cover from the drone, and you can do a U-turn"

"Good idea." Dakota brought the car to a stop under the bridge.

Talking into her phone, Afton said, "Yes, I'm with Dakota Knox, the missing young man, and we are being chased by an armed drone. . . . No . . . Yes. We just stopped under a bridge."

As she said those words, the large black drone descended into their view about fifty feet in front of the Lamborghini.

Dakota said, "We're clear for a U-turn. Hold on, you two!" He cranked the steering wheel to the right and pressed down on the gas pedal. The Lamborghini growled and took off. A few seconds later, they were going eighty miles an hour in the other direction.

"Faster!" Hank yelled, looking out the window.

Dakota looked down at the speedometer: 142 mph.

"In a quarter-mile, turn left for the police station," Afton said.

Dakota slowed the car down and made the left.

"Okay," Afton said, "we'll be turning right in one mile."

"Hank, do you see the drone in your mirror?"

"No. I think we lost it, or it turned around."

Dakota breathed a sigh of relief.

"All right," Afton said to the police dispatcher, "we'll be pulling into the police station in about one minute. . . . Okay, thanks. Bye." Afton turned to Dakota. "Two officers will be waiting out front for us. . . . There's the station on the right. It looks open."

Dakota pulled the Lamborghini into the parking lot and opened the doors. The three teens stepped out and were greeted by two friendly police officers, who walked them toward the building's entrance.

"I don't see the drone. You must have lost it," an officer said to Dakota.

"Yeah, I hope so," Dakota said, looking up to the sky.

When they reached the glass doors, Dakota stopped. "I'm sorry. I forgot something in the car. I'll be right back."

He opened the car door, reached behind the seat, and pulled out the Pontius Pilate stone. *I don't want to leave this unattended.*

Inside the building, a detective questioned Dakota about the kidnappers. Afton described the house's location to another officer, and Hank was on the phone explaining what had transpired to Abigail.

"Oh, no," Dakota said. "Hear that?"

"What?" the detective asked.

"That humming . . . that buzzing sound—the drone is back! They must be tracking the location of the **Lamborghini**."

The detective stood and walked down the hall toward the building's main entrance. As he neared the reception area, the glass windows were blown apart by a hail of gunfire.

Dakota, Afton, and Hank looked wide-eyed at each other.

"Get under the desk," Dakota said. He peeked down the hall. Officers were yelling and scrambling for cover as the reception area was being shredded by bullets.

Dakota ran down the hall away from the gunfire, looking for an alternative exit. He found one, went outside, and peeked around the corner toward the front of the building. The drone was shooting up the entrance from about thirty feet high. It

stopped a few seconds later.

*Is it out of ammo?*

The drone slowly descended to about twelve feet above the ground and turned.

*Whoever's flying that thing is trying to get a better angle.*

Dakota took out Radomir's pistol from his back pocket. He pulled the slide back and could see a live round in the chamber.

*That's one shot.*

He released the clip to see how many bullets remained in the gun.

*Probably about ten shots. I'm thankful my dad taught me how to use a gun. David took Goliath down with a single stone. Help me to aim well, God.*

Dakota jammed the clip back into the gun and dashed toward the drone. He rolled down onto the asphalt directly under the drone and pointed the gun at its underbelly. Poom! Poom! Poom! He fired five or six shots. Then he aimed at a propeller support arm and fired more shots until the clip was out.

He quickly rolled away and got to his feet, hoping the drone would crash.

It didn't.

It began to rotate counterclockwise and tilt.

*Oh, no. It's going to fire at me!* Dakota ran and hid behind the Lamborghini.

*Lord, what should I do if that thing starts firing at the car? Where should I go?* He felt his heart thumping underneath his rib cage.

The drone was getting closer and

194

lower. *Oh, Lord, Jesus!* He imagined bullets tearing the car and him apart any second. He heard metal begin to tweak and bend. *It's happening—the drone is shooting up the other side of the car. I'm done.*

Dakota closed his eyes. *Into Your hands, I commit my spirit, Lord.* The hullabaloo of noise and flying shrapnel sounded like someone turned on a blender full of forks.

Then there was silence.

Dakota opened his eyes. *I'm alive?* He felt his chest to make sure. *I am alive!* He crawled toward the front of the Lamborghini to survey the parking lot. The drone was on its side, surrounded by shards of its propellers and support arms.

*The drone is down—hallelujah!* Dakota breathed out in relief. *Thank You, God.* He stood and walked to the other side of the car. *Not a single bullet hole. Wow. The noise must have been the drone falling apart when it crashed.*

Dakota headed toward the station's shattered entrance.

An officer walked out through the broken pieces of glass. "Great shooting, kid. I'm glad you're okay. Two things I need from you."

"What's that?"

"Number one, knuckles."

Dakota gave him a fist bump with a big smile.

"Number two, the gun."

"It's over there by the Lamborghini."

"Is the gun yours?"

"No, I took it from one of the kidnappers. I think his name is Radomir."

Dakota heard shoes crunching across the broken glass off to his side. He turned. It was Afton. She stretched out her arms, and the two hugged.

Afton looked into his eyes. "I'm so glad you're okay."

"Thanks. I'm glad *you're* okay."

"I heard an officer inside say that the drone crashed."

"It did."

"That's a relief."

Hank walked over. "That was awesome, Dak! I saw what you did on the camera monitor in the detective's office. You shot it down!"

"Well, that might have had something to do with it crashing."

An officer walked over. "I think that had *everything* to do with it crashing. Why don't you guys come back inside with me? We need to finish debriefing Dakota, get some information on the kidnappers, and so on."

A while later, there was a happy and emotional reunion in the parking lot when Dakota and Afton's families showed up.

A police officer walked over. "Sorry to interrupt you, Knox and Hansley families. I have an update for you—great news. Our officers arrested four men and one woman at the estate. And, as you said in the interview earlier, Dakota, there's a gold-mine of artifacts and paintings in the house—definitely some stolen pieces. But the house is secured and sealed off. We'll bring in museum curators and artifact experts tomorrow."

"That's awesome news," Dakota said. "Thank you. I'd like to put in a good word for the woman. Her name is Sabiya. I wouldn't be alive if it weren't for her. She brought me food and water and helped me get free. I don't think she's done anything wrong. Please treat her kindly."

"I'll let the officers know that. Thank you. Well, we're done here. Get this young man home. He needs a shower and probably a hot meal."

"That sounds amazing," Dakota said. "I've been wearing the same clothes for I don't know how many days—too many."

"Yes. Let's get you home and cleaned up," Abigail said. "I'll order some pizzas and salads, and whoever would like can come and eat at our place."

"That sounds amazing!" Hank said. Everyone agreed.

Hank started walking over to the Lamborghini and yelled, "Shotgun!"

Several people in the parking lot turned and looked in alarm.

An officer yelled, "Everybody down!"

Hank bent down a bit. "What?"

The officer asked him, "Where's the person with the shotgun?"

Hank laughed. "No, I said 'shotgun'—it's slang in the U.S. for 'I get the front passenger seat.'"

"Oh, okay." The officer put his gun back in its holster. "Probably not a good word to use at a police station after a shooting."

"Ooh, I'm sorry," Hank said. "But Dakota, I'm driving back with you, right?"

"Uh, Hank, we don't get to keep the Lamborghini."

"Oh. I thought you got to keep anything you escaped with if the criminals tried to kill you. Finders keepers, losers weepers—something like that. No?"

"No, Hank. That's not quite how it works."

"Like, it's not a *U.K.* thing?"

"Like it's not an *adult* thing . . . anywhere," Dakota said.

"Oh, you're not an adult yet though, technically, so—"

"That reminds me," Dakota said to the officer, "here are the keys."

"Thank you."

William Knox, Dakota's dad, put his arm around Dakota's shoulder and pulled him in tight. "What a happy reunion this is, son. We're elated that you're alive. You're a little dinged up, but you'll be okay."

"Yeah, I'll be okay. I'm glad to see you, Dad. Missed you. Did Light Shield let you have a few days off?"

"For a missing son? Absolutely! Hey, Dakota, I'm really proud of you. How you survived, how you escaped . . . your godly character. You blow me away, Dak."

"Thanks, Dad. I give God all the credit."

# Chapter 32
## Sunday morning, June 26, Marylebone.

The next morning, Dakota strolled out of his bedroom a little after 10 a.m.

"There he is! How'd you sleep?" his dad asked.

"Okay. I had a couple of bad dreams . . . being chased by dogs . . . getting shot at. But I got some sleep."

"I'm sorry, Dakota. I'm sure bad dreams are normal after such a horrible ordeal," Abigail said.

Jalynn walked into the kitchen. "I bet some of Dad's waffles would help you feel better."

"You made waffles, Dad?"

"Just for you, bud."

"That's nice of you. Thanks. I'll definitely have a couple."

"I'll bring them to you, Dak," Jalynn said. "With syrup and peanut butter on them, right?"

"Right, Jay. Thanks. Afton's coming over to eat breakfast with me. Can you make two plates?"

"Two plates of waffles and fruit coming up."

Dakota sat down on the couch. "Wow, I really missed you guys. I thought I might never see you again."

Abigail sat down next to him. "We missed you too."

Hank rinsed off his plate in the kitchen sink. "I can't believe they put you in a cage, Dak. That's horrible."

"I hope they're locked up for life," Abigail said.

William agreed. "So do I."

"They deserve the *death* penalty," Dakota said. "Sabiya, the maid there, told me they've murdered people and buried them on the property."

"That's awful. So evil," Abigail said.

"On a happier note," Dakota said, "what are your thoughts about returning to Israel? Now that we know the thieves live *here* and have all been arrested, it's probably safe to go back, huh, Dad?"

"Well, we want to leave that up to you, Dak. I'm under contract with Light Shield, so I have to go back. But Mom and I are wondering if you'd like to return to California or stay a little longer here in London. We want to do whatever will bless you."

"Oh, that's nice of you guys. I'd love to go back to Israel if the Hansleys are going back. We were having such a good time there."

"I texted with Mrs. Hansley this morning, and they are for sure going back."

"Then count me in!"

Hank and Jalynn gave each other a high five.

"All right," Abigail said, "we'll finish the summer at the beach house in Herzliya."

"We should stay in London for at least a few more days," Dakota said. "You guys have hardly done any sightseeing."

"I'd love that," Abigail said.

There was a knock on the door. Dakota hopped up. "It's Afton." He opened the door. "Good morning, pretty girl. How is Miss Hansley doing on this beautiful morning?"

"Very good, and you, Mr. Knox?"

"Much better after a shower, some good food, and some sleep. Do you like waffles?"

"Love them!"

"Good, come in."

A delivery man walked up as Afton headed in. "I have a delivery for a Dakota Knox."

Dakota signed for the box and brought it in. "It was shipped priority overnight from Scotland Yard."

"Scotland Yard? What's that?" Jalynn asked.

"It's the name of London's police department," Afton said.

Dakota opened the box and read a handwritten note:

> *Dakota, we heard your phone was lost during your unfortunate ordeal. Several officers pitched in, and we bought you a new iPhone. We hope you enjoy it!*
> *–Your friends at Scotland Yard.*

"Wow. That's so nice. And it's the newest model."

"That is so kind of them," Afton said.

Dakota and Afton sat at the dining table and enjoyed breakfast together.

"Great waffles, Dad. Thanks."

"And a big thanks to whoever cut up all these strawberries, bananas, mangoes, and blueberries. So yum." Afton said.

When they were done eating, Dakota opened his new phone. He signed into his Apple account and noticed that all the photos he thought he had lost on his old phone were downloading into his photo folder.

"Oh, wow, Afton. I thought I had lost all these photos of us in Israel. But they were all backed up in the cloud!"

"Praise God."

"These are priceless memories of us at Megiddo, Galilee, Ein Gedi, the Dead Sea, Qumran, Caesarea, Jerusalem. I'm so thankful for these pics! I don't ever want to forget these special days, falling in love with you."

"Such a sweet time, Mr. Knox."

"I should listen to this voicemail. Excuse me for a second." A couple of minutes later, Dakota stood. "Hey guys, I just listened to a voicemail from one of the detectives working on the case. He said curators from the British Museum are at the estate this morning and have identified and secured the Isaiah Scroll, the **crucifixion heel**, and **Caiaphas's ossuary**! Isn't that amazing?"

Afton said, "That means all the artifacts stolen from the Israel Museum have been recovered."

"So amazing!" Abigail said.

Dakota continued. "They've also identified other stolen artifacts and paintings that have been missing for years."

"That's incredible!" William said.

It was a happy day for the Knoxes.

They ended the day by walking with the Hansleys to their Sunday evening church service. The pastor taught on the words of the apostle Paul in Romans 8:28 . . .

> And we know that God causes all things to work together for good to those who love God, to those who are called according to His purpose.

# Chapter 33
## Tuesday, July 5, Herzliya, Israel.

Nine days later, the Knox and Hansley kids were back in Israel swimming in the **lagoon-style pool** at the Knoxes' beach house. Dakota and Afton stood near the waterfall on top of a rock ledge.

Dakota took hold of Afton's hand. "On the count of three, we jump. Okay?"

"Okay."

"One, two, three!"

The two teenagers splashed into the warm pool water and slowly floated to the surface with the bubbles. Afton said, "What a blessing to be back in this warm weather."

"Such a blessing," Dakota said. "I love Israel, this house, the beach, and I love you!"

"I love you too, Dakota! Hey, if school starts on August 22, what should—"

"Sorry to interrupt you, Afton." Abigail walked out and bent down by the edge of the pool. "Dakota, the secretary for the Prime Minister of Israel, Nathaniel Efron, is on the phone. She'd like to connect you on a phone call with him."

"Okay. Wow. I'll get out." Dakota climbed out of the pool, dried his hands, and took the phone from his mom. "Hello, this is Dakota."

"Hi Dakota, I'm Prime Minister Nathaniel Efron's secretary. We spoke a couple of weeks ago when you and your family visited Balfour. Thanks for taking his call. Please hold."

A couple of minutes later, the Prime Minister said, "Do I have the pleasure of speaking to Dakota Knox?"

"Yes, this is Dakota. How are you, Prime Minister?"

"Very well, thank you."

"I heard about what you endured at the hands of those men in England. We're praying for a full recovery."

"Thank you."

"How are you feeling?"

"Great. My bruises and cuts are healing pretty good."

"Glad to hear that, Dakota. I've been told that the stolen artifacts are all safely back in the hands of our museum curators. I wanted to call you and personally thank you for your help in their recovery. This is some of the best news Israelis have heard all year. Those artifacts are part of our history and will be a tremendous blessing to people who visit the museum for years to come."

"You're welcome. I give all the credit for their safe recovery to God."

"I know you do. You're a humble young man. And we're so pleased to know that the thieves have been arrested and will be brought to justice."

"So am I."

"Now, Dakota, you and your family were here in my office a couple of weeks ago when we talked about the recovery of the **David Inscription**. 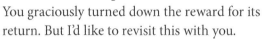 You graciously turned down the reward for its return. But I'd like to revisit this with you.

"I talked to the museum director and members of the Knesset, and they all agreed that it would be an honor for us to give the designated reward money to you. The museum receives millions of dollars every year from donors and philanthropic foundations. So, giving the reward money to you isn't going to hurt the museum's operating budget or lead to any layoffs. It also might help the museum with good PR.

"So, I want to encourage you to receive it. Maybe you could use it to pay for college or buy a car. What do you think?"

"Wow. Well, um, Prime Minister Efron, I wasn't expecting this, but yeah, I guess I'll take it. I don't feel like I deserve it, but—"

"Oh, you deserve it. You nearly died at the hands of those evil men, and you somehow managed to escape with the Pontius Pilate artifact in your hands. You are more than deserving."

"Well, thank you, Prime Minister."

"Okay, wonderful. I'll have the check made out to you and delivered to the house there in Herzliya later today. Sound good?"

"Yes, thank you!"

"Give my warmest regards to your family. It was a delight meeting them a couple of weeks ago. Take care."

"Take care, God bless."

"God bless you, Dakota."

Dakota handed the phone back to his mom. "Wow. They really want to give the reward money to me. So, I said, yes."

"Well," Abigail said, "I know your reasons for turning it down before, Dakota. But if anyone deserves it, it's you. I'm glad you agreed to it."

Dakota looked down at Afton in the pool. She smiled and nodded. "I agree, Dakota. After all you've been through, receive it as a blessing from the Lord."

"How much is the reward?" Hank asked.

"I don't know. I didn't ask. I think it's for a lot."

Later that afternoon, a courier knocked on the door with an envelope in his hand. Dakota signed the man's tablet to confirm the delivery.

"I think I'd like to open it by myself in my room."

"That's fine, honey," Abigail said.

Dakota walked into his room, knelt with the envelope in his hands, and silently prayed. *Heavenly Father, thank You from the bottom of my heart for keeping me alive through that horrible time. What a trial! But You were with me. You helped me escape. You helped me recover the Pontius Pilate artifact. I give You all the glory, praise, and honor. I don't know how much this check is for. I think it's a lot, but before I open it, I want to dedicate it all back to You. I'm going to give ten percent of it to my home church and other Christian ministries that are spreading the gospel. That's the least I can do. Give me wisdom with the rest. I'll need a car in Virginia. I'd like to pay for my college education to take that burden off my parents. I'd like to give a big chunk to Afton and some to Hank and Jalynn. I'd like to help Sabiya find a new place to live. So, guide me; help me be a good steward, Father. And it's in Jesus's name I pray, Amen.*

He carefully opened the envelope and pulled out the check. *Whoa! 5,000,000 shekels?*

He pulled out his phone and converted it into U.S. dollars: $1,495,000.

*Almost 1.5 million dollars.* "Wow!" *That will cover college, and a car, and Afton's college, and . . . wisdom needed.*

He walked out of his room with a big smile and showed his family the check. Everyone was blown away.

"You're a millionaire, Dakota? Wow!" Jalynn said.

"You could buy one of those Lamborghini Aventador's for about $550,000 and still have money left over," Hank said. "That's what I'd do."

"Oh, I know you'd do that, Hank. And you'd crash it the first day!"


Dakota and Afton spent the next few weeks in Israel doing all their favorite things: surfing and snorkeling at Herzliya,

walking along the boardwalk for ice cream, exploring archaeological sites, swimming and lounging by the pool with good
books, riding **beach cruisers**, watching movies, driving the
Bronco with the top off, playing billiards in the game room,
enjoying meals together, and worshipping with Dakota's guitar
by the firepit in the evenings.

Dakota and Afton's love for each other grew by the day.

# Chapter 34
## Monday, August 22
## Liberty University, Virginia.

Ten days after saying goodbye at the airport in Israel, Dakota and Afton were reunited at **Liberty University** when they moved into their dorms. On Monday, the first day of school, they met at the school's dining hall for lunch.

"How's your day been?" Dakota asked.

"Really good. I loved both of my classes."

"Oh, good!"

"Yeah, having Christian professors is amazing. My history professor asked if anyone had any prayer requests. How cool is that?"

"Super cool. Have you gotten to know your roommates a little better?"

"Yes, they are really sweet girls. How about you, Dakota?"

"Yeah, the guys are fine—still getting to know them. I'm used to having my own room, so it's going to take a little adjusting. One of the guys snores really bad, but what do I do?"

"Get some ear plugs."

"I need to."

Dakota and Afton sat down at a table and prayed for their meal.

"How was your intro to archaeology class?" Dakota asked.

"Amazing. Learned a lot already. And get this. Next spring break, I have the option of going to Jordan for seven days to help with an archaeological excavation."

"That would be so cool. Where at?"

"A site that archaeologists believe is the ancient city of Sodom."

"Really! As in Sodom, one of the cities that God rained down fire on in the Book of Genesis?"

"Yeah, it's about eight miles northeast of the Dead Sea."

"They found it?"

"They think so—the ruins of the ancient city line up with all the geographical details in the Bible. What I found most interesting, though, was that the city was destroyed by intense heat. Archaeologists have discovered a wealth of evidence that the city was obliterated by a sudden blast of heat."

"Whoa!"

Afton took a sip of her iced tea. "The destruction and ash layer left behind is a meter thick in some areas and contains charred human remains and pieces of melted pottery that had been exposed to temperatures over 2,000 degrees Fahrenheit!"

"Yikes—that's hot."

"The destruction of the city was so thorough that the entire area remained without human settlements for the next 500–700 years. Archaeologists have also made a compelling case that the city was destroyed within the right window of time, the Middle Bronze Age between 2100–1550 BC when Abraham and Lot lived. But there's much more to discover there, and our class has been invited to help."

"That's so cool, Afton. You should go."

"I'd like to."

"What a great experience that would be for you to work on an actual site!"

"I think so. You should come too, Dakota. I'm sure my professor would allow you to. I told him after class that you were the one who helped return the stolen artifacts to the museum over the summer, and he was floored. He asked if I thought you might come and talk to our class sometime. I said, probably. So, I'm sure he'd love it if you went to Jordan with the class."

"Maybe I *will* come."

When they finished eating, they strolled back toward their dorms.

"I love being here in America," Afton said. "I love going to a Christian college. And how cool are all these hills and trees around the campus?"

"I'm so glad you're enjoying the U.S. and school. Are we on for our date later?"

"For sure. Three thirty?"

"Yes! It's going to be a fancy dinner, so feel free to dress up. And oh, yeah, bring a sweater or jacket. We'll probably spend some time outside, and I'd hate for you to be cold."

Dakota walked her back to her female-only residence hall.

Afton swiped her badge to open the door. "I'll see you at three thirty."

"Can't wait! See you then."

# Chapter 35

A couple of hours later, Dakota waited outside Afton's dormitory. He pulled up the left sleeve of his dark gray sports coat and looked at his watch. At three thirty, Afton walked out the door in a black dress. *Oh, my goodness. She's the prettiest girl on campus. Wow!*

He stood and handed her a long-stemmed red rose. "Well, good afternoon, Miss Hansley. You look lovely."

"Thank you. And you look very handsome in your jeans and sports coat."

"Thanks. How are you?"

"Wonderful!"

"Ready for a fun evening?"

"Absolutely. You?"

"I can hardly wait. Let's go."

They held hands and walked to the parking lot.

"Did you borrow a friend's car?" Afton asked.

"Uh, no." Dakota reached into his pocket and pressed a button on a key fob.

"I thought we'd just take this." Dakota stopped next to a brand-new dark-silver Ford Bronco.

Afton laughed. "Yeah, right, like we were back in Israel."

"No, I'm serious," Dakota said. "It's mine."

"This is yours?"

"I bought it yesterday."

"Seriously? Dakota! This is amazing."

"Hop in, Miss Hansley." He helped her into the car and shut her door.

"Wow! I love the color you chose."

"So do I. I enjoyed driving the Bronco so much in Israel, I thought with some of the reward money, I'd buy my own."

"What a blessing."

As they drove east, they enjoyed looking at the trees and green hills along the highway that connects Lynchburg and Chesapeake, Virginia.

"This is so different than London!" Afton said. "So much open land. Wow!"

"It's a lot different than San Diego too!" Dakota added. "Not a city or billboard for miles and miles. You can breathe here—I love it."

When they got to the coastal city of Portsmouth, Dakota said, "Okay, put your hand over your eyes. I'd like to surprise you."

"Okay, I can't see a thing."

Dakota pulled the Bronco into a parking lot at the Tide-water Yacht Marina and turned off the car. "Keep your eyes closed." He hopped out and opened her door. "Here, take my hand, and I'll lead you."

"I hear seagulls and smell saltwater."

"You are so perceptive, Miss Hansley."

He led her to a dock where dozens of boats were moored. "Do you remember when we went for coffee at the marina in Israel, and you said, 'Wouldn't it be great if you had one of these yachts?'"

Afton nodded her head. "Yes."

"Well, I don't know if you prayed for that. But I think God heard someone's prayer because now I have one!"

"You do?"

"I do! Go ahead and open your eyes."

In front of Afton was a beautiful white yacht more than a hundred feet long.

Afton bent down and looked at Dakota. "What! This is *yours?* You bought this with the reward money?"

"Oh, no. The reward money wouldn't be enough for this."

"It was a gift."

"What!" Afton said with a huge smile.

"Do you remember those news interviews I did in London a few weeks ago about recovering the artifacts?"

"Of course."

"Well, an older man, Walter Pembleton, contacted me after-ward. He's a wealthy Christian businessman and art collector who lives in England. He had a few paintings stolen from his home a few years ago. But museum curators found them in Radomir's collection and returned them to him."

"I bet that made him happy!"

"He was so happy. Well, a couple of weeks ago, he bought a bunch of stuff at an auction of Radomir's estate, including this yacht, some cars, and paintings. But then Mr. Pembleton saw one of my interviews. When he heard about the beach shooting in Israel and the kidnapping in London, he said his heart was moved to bless me. So, he prayed about what to do. And he believes God put it in his heart to give *me* the yacht."

"That's amazing!"

"So, he emailed me and asked if I'd like it. I thought this *can't* be real—this must be a scam. But my parents checked it out with the police, and they verified that he was a real person and that he had bought it. So I called Mr. Pembleton, thanked him, and told him I'd love it. He said, 'I only ask one thing of you—use it to bring glory to God like you've been doing in these interviews with the press.' Can you believe?"

"Wow, Dakota. That's incredible."

"But it gets better."

"He said he'd have it detailed top to bottom and sailed over to the U.S. And get this. He said he'd even cover the expenses of having it moored and maintained."

"That's so crazy amazing!"

"So I'm going to have it moored here. And I wanted you to be the first person, besides my parents, to see it."

"Well, I'm honored, Dakota."

"*I'm* honored to have you for my girlfriend. And while we're here, I thought we'd have dinner on board."

"That sounds lovely, Mr. Knox."

"Let's go check it out." Dakota led her across a ramp and onto the boat.

As they walked around, Afton said, "Whoa. This is super nice . . . gorgeous . . . I'm blown away . . . unbelievable!"

"So, it has three levels, an outdoor hot tub and fireplace over here, all these comfortable outdoor seats, a spacious living room inside here, this beautiful kitchen. It has bedrooms and beds down below with enough room to sleep up to twenty people."

"It's like a floating multi-million-dollar house, Dakota. Wow. Do you know how to sail it?"

"Not at all."

They both laughed.

"The little bit I know about sailing, I learned watching reruns of *Gilligan's Island*. And, uh, that didn't end well."

Afton laughed. "No, it didn't."

"But I'll learn! For tonight, I hired a guy to sail us around the Chesapeake Bay for a sunset cruise. I also hired a chef and one of his assistants to make and serve dinner."

"Oh, my goodness, Dakota!"

"Come up here."

He led her up the stairs to the yacht's dining room where there was a round wooden table with elegant plates, flowers, and lit candles.

"We'll be having dinner here when it's ready."

"Wow, Dakota. I thought our dinner at The Shard was nice, but you've taken it up to another level. Truly amazing. How good is our God to deliver you out of Radomir's hands and then give his yacht to *you!* This is so crazy."

"God is good! And I want to use this boat for good. I'm praying for wisdom and ideas about that, but in the meantime, let's sail."

"Let's!"

"I'll go tell the captain we're ready. And I think I'll put some music on. What are you in the mood for?"

"Hmm . . . jazzy big band music would be fun."

"You got it."

Minutes later, the massive **yacht** was gliding through the glassy water. Dakota and Afton sat on an outdoor couch, enjoying the scenery along the Elizabeth River and Chesapeake Bay.

"I don't think we'll need our jackets with this warm weather."

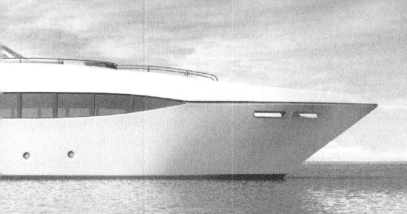

"It's perfect out," Afton said.

A waiter approached with drinks in glass goblets. "May I interest you in a pineapple juice with fresh mint and lime?"

"Yes, please."

"Thank you."

"It's delicious," Afton said. "What a lovely evening, Dakota. Thank you for arranging all this."

"You're welcome."

"This is a little more relaxing than our last boat ride in London."

Dakota laughed. "I'd say so."

A few minutes later, the waiter informed them that dinner was ready. They walked down to the dining room. Dakota pulled out Afton's chair, and they sat down.

The chef said, "Welcome, Mr. Knox and Miss Hansley. It is a pleasure to cook for you both tonight. There are three entrées to choose from. Here, we have wild Alaskan salmon with lemon, butter, and capers with sautéed asparagus and mashed potatoes. Over here, we have maple-glazed Manchester quail, chestnut gnocchi with sautéed garlic, and olive oil spinach. And here, we have a tomahawk rib-eye steak with sautéed mushrooms."

"This all looks and smells amazing," Dakota said. "Thank you, Dennis."

Dakota prayed for the meal, and the two agreed to share a little bit of everything.

As they savored the delicious food in the warm hues of the setting sun, they laughed, reminisced about meeting each other, and talked about what the future might hold.

"Afton, I love you with all my heart. We're a bit too young to get married. I think our parents would fall over if I proposed to you, and we wouldn't want that. But I want you to know that I want to spend the rest of my life with you. I am head-over-heels in love with you."

"I feel the same about you."

Dakota continued. "I would love to be your husband when the time is right. I want to be there to care for you, encourage you, and support you and the archaeological work you'll be doing. I'd love to sail around the world with you and explore places, and maybe instead of staying at a hotel while you're working on excavations, we could live on this yacht."

"Dakota, being married to you would be amazing. I love you more than I thought was humanly possible. God will give us wisdom as to the timing. And this boat—yes, it would be an amazing home away from home."

Dakota took a sip of his pineapple juice. "I'm not sure where our home base would be. We can figure that out down the road. And I'm still planning on finishing my education and training in criminal justice. But the more I think about joining Homeland Security when I'm done, the more I lean towards *not* doing that."

"Really?"

"Yeah. I think I'd prefer to run my own business so that I can have the flexibility to travel and support you when you're working on excavations."

"I'd love that. What kind of business are you thinking of starting?"

"I'm thinking of maybe opening a private investigation firm."

"The next Sherlock Holmes! Dakota, that seems like a job

you'd *love*. And you'd be your own boss and could make your own schedule. And having you close by would be a dream."

"Well, I trust God will direct our steps, won't He?"

"I'm confident of that," Afton said.

The chef walked to their table. "Are you two ready for dessert?"

"Yes, thank you, Dennis. And dinner was absolutely astounding," Dakota said. Afton nodded in agreement.

"I'm so glad you liked it. I'll be back in a few minutes with a warm chocolate lava cake and vanilla ice cream."

Afton looked up at the speaker in the ceiling above them. "I love this song."

"I do too. It's on my big band playlist."

"It's an oldie."

"Yeah, it's Bobby Darin. I think it was recorded in the sixties."

"Let's dance, Dakota."

"I would be honored, Miss Hansley."

He took her hand and led her to the outdoor deck. The sun had set, but the colorful afterglow and warm air lingered over the Chesapeake Bay. The two smiling teenagers danced and laughed while Bobby Darin's upbeat classic **"More"** played . . .

More than the greatest love the world has known,
This is the love that I give to you, alone
More than the simple words I try to say,
I only live to love you more each day

More than you'll ever know,
My arms long to hold you so

My life will be in your keeping;
Waking, sleeping, laughing, weeping

Longer than always is a long, long time
But far beyond forever, you'll be mine
I know I never lived before, and my heart is very sure
No one else could love you more

The chef poked his head outside when the song ended. "Your dessert is ready . . . whenever you are. Take your time."

"Thank you, Dennis."

"Dancing was fun, Dakota."

"That was. We can dance some more later. Let's have some **lava cake**!"

They sat next to each other at the dining table and dug their spoons into the warm chocolate cake and ice cream. After a couple of bites, Dakota accidentally dropped his spoon on the floor.

"Ah, shoot!"

"No worries," Afton said. "We can use mine . . . if you don't mind my cooties."

"Your cooties!" Dakota laughed. "I *like* your cooties."

"You do?"

"Yeah, watch." He scooped some cake and ice cream with Afton's spoon, placed it in his mouth, and pulled it out clean. "Delicious! But now it has *my* cooties on it."

"So gross. I'm not touching it now!" Afton said laughingly. "I'm kidding. Feed me a bite, cutie."

He scooped some of the chocolate confection and vanilla ice cream and guided it into Afton's mouth. As she began to remove the dessert with her lips, he slowly pulled the spoon back while it was still in her mouth.

As her face got closer to his, Dakota said, "I love you, Afton Hansley." When her face was a couple of inches from his, Dakota slid the spoon out of her mouth and dropped it to the floor.

They had held off kissing from the night Dakota asked Afton to be his girlfriend in London. But the time had come. They were committed to each other. They loved each other deeply, and their supreme desire was to please God.

Dakota had thought that when the time was right, he would *ask* if he could kiss her. But on this balmy night, under the twinkling stars on the Chesapeake Bay, no words were necessary.

Their lips touched for the very first time.

Short, gentle kisses quickly morphed into a long passionate one as their lips locked on to each other. As the kissing continued, they stood, caressed each other's cheeks, ears, and necks with their fingers, and ran their hands through each other's hair.

"Wow," Afton said softly as she rested her forehead against Dakota's.

"That was amazing," Dakota whispered. "I've never kissed anyone. So I don't know if I'm doing it right or—"

"Shh." Afton placed her finger on his lips. "That kiss was wonderful."

"You think?"

Looking up into his blue eyes, Afton said, "Actually, no."

"No?"

"I think you need more practice, Dakota. *Lots* of practice. Kiss me again, please."

They kissed again . . . and again.

"Let's go sit outside by the fire," Dakota said.

They walked outside and sat on the couch. Dakota put his arm around Afton as she snuggled up against him. The orange glow of the flickering flames danced across their faces.

"Those kisses, Dakota . . . I don't think I'll ever be able to eat chocolate cake again without remembering our first kiss on the Chesapeake Bay. I love you."

"I love you, Afton. Sitting here on this amazing yacht with the girl of my dreams . . . a billion stars overhead, the sound of the moonlit water lapping up against the side of the boat . . . all I can say is, 'Now to Him who is able to do exceedingly abundantly above all that we ask or think . . . to Him be the glory forever and ever.'"

"Ephesians three. I love those verses. God has been so good to us, Dakota."

"He has."

At the end of the evening, Dakota walked Afton back to the reception area of the girls' dorm.

"Dakota, that was the loveliest evening ever. Thank you for everything. Bike ride and coffee in the morning? I don't have class until eleven o'clock."

"I'd love that. Text me in the morning."

"I will."

"Sleep well, my love."

"Sleep well, cutie. I love you!"

They kissed one more time.

Dakota turned around and walked to his dorm. *Thank You, God! You have blessed me so much. I truly feel like the happiest guy on the planet.*

**Continue following Dakota and Afton in Book 3!**

*Did you enjoy this book? Please consider posting a rating or brief review at Amazon.com or ABR-store.com. Thank you! I'd love to hear your feedback. Email me at:* **Charlie@AlwaysBeReady.com**

Made in the USA
Las Vegas, NV
03 July 2024

91831135R00132